---------------- ★ ----------------

I folded my arms across my chest, carefully keeping the bruised one away from Grant. "Was starting a riot part of the game plan? It would have been nice if someone had warned me."

"We didn't know how much we could tell you. Then you missed the meeting—"

"Next time I miss a meeting, I'll get a note from my mother. Roz already jumped down my throat because I don't spend every minute of my life at WARM headquarters. What's her problem?"

"Roz always worries that every newcomer is a government spy. Don't worry, she'll loosen up—unless you *are* a cop."

---------------- ★ ----------------

"Blaine is a feisty female sleuth, well paired with her sister Eileen."

—*Publishers Weekly*

"Blaine . . . is a fearless investigator."
—*New York Times Book Review*

Sharon Zukowski

Dancing in the Dark

WORLDWIDE.

TORONTO • NEW YORK • LONDON
AMSTERDAM • PARIS • SYDNEY • HAMBURG
STOCKHOLM • ATHENS • TOKYO • MILAN
MADRID • WARSAW • BUDAPEST • AUCKLAND

To my mother, Helen Meyers, who's always been my number one fan

DANCING IN THE DARK

A Worldwide Mystery/July 1994

First published by St. Martin's Press, Incorporated.

ISBN 0-373-26148-9

Grateful acknowledgment is made by the publisher for permission to reprint lyrics from the following song: "If Wishes Were Changes"— words, Nanci Griffith; music, Nanci Griffith and James Hooker. Copyright © 1989 Irving Music, Inc. (BMI), and Rick Hall Music, Inc. (ASCAP). All rights on behalf of Ponder Heart Music administered by Irving Music, Inc. All rights reserved.

ACKNOWLEDGMENTS

My overdue thanks for encouragement,
support, advice, and good humor go to
Elizabeth Cavanaugh, my patient agent;
Pete Meyers, Sr.; and Barbara Van Benschoten.
Special thanks to my sister, Leeann Zukowski,
for trying to keep me organized.

ONE

I HATE MORNING meetings and reserve an extra measure of hatred for Monday morning meetings—they always bring me trouble. This one was no exception.

It started on a sour note when my prospective client asked, "When are the men coming?" He frowned with disappointment when he learned that Blaine Stewart was female. The frown deepened when I informed him that no men would be in attendance. He muttered something about women's liberation and launched into his tale before I could react. Things got worse from there.

The man's deep voice droned on. The novelty of his Texas drawl wore off after a few minutes. His stories of cattle roundups ceased to be amusing but my attempts to guide his conversation to business were ineffective. My coffee cup was empty. I decided to leave it empty; Jacob Faradeux wasn't accustomed to being interrupted, certainly not by someone in need of a fourth cup of coffee. Rather than find myself on the receiving end of another withering glare, I sat back and tried to look like the alert investigator Faradeux wanted to hire.

"Trouble is, no one has the balls to stand up to these people. Benji, my oldest boy, is a crybaby wimp. His brother, Paul, is lazy. He'd sit on his butt and watch TV all day if I didn't make him work for a living. They say I should listen to those people, negotiate with them."

Faradeux gestured to the woman sitting at his side. "Nanci here is the only one with balls—and she's a girl."

Disapproval was etched in his voice. Faradeux couldn't admit that his sons hadn't inherited his strengths, and he certainly wouldn't admit that his favorite child was a woman. Women weren't held in high esteem by Faradeux.

Nanci, who was at least thirty years past the age of girlhood, grabbed his arm in an attempt to stop the tirade. Faradeux ignored her gesture.

I gave up being polite; I needed another jolt of caffeine. I walked across the room to the coffee urn set on a small table in the corner, filled my cup, and rudely said, "Get to the point, Mr. Faradeux. I don't have time to listen to your family problems."

"Red, I've been telling you why I need to hire your firm. Haven't you been listening?" Faradeux's face was pink with anger; his dark eyes challenged me to respond to the taunt.

People have called me "Red" all my life. I can't understand why they think it's such a grave insult—I like my red hair. I took a sip of coffee and said, "You've been telling me wonderful stories about Texas, your ranch, your company, and your family. Why don't you tell me why you want to hire me? And don't call me Red again or I'll be forced to call you contumacious and throw you the hell out of here."

Faradeux threw his head back and laughed. The bellow rolled through the conference room, bounced off the far wall, and came back to us. He finally caught his breath and said, "I like you. Don't know if you're complimenting me or insulting me and I don't wanna know."

"Mr. Faradeux—"

"Call me Jacob."

"Jacob, what's your problem? Why can't someone in Texas handle it?"

Faradeux drawled, "If my problem was in Texas I wouldn't be needing your help, I'd know how to deal with it. My problems are right here in Manhattan."

He started another meandering history of scraping his empire from the grassy high plains of Texas, battling sandstorms, flash floods, and "Blue Northers" from the Rockies that brought freezing wind, ice, and snow. I looked at his daughter, silently appealing for her intercession.

Nanci grimaced, opened her briefcase, and removed a green file folder. She placed the file on the table, folded her hands, and waited. Blond and tanned, Nanci was a petite, female version of Jacob Faradeux, except his fingernails weren't long and elegantly manicured.

Jacob paused. His daughter said quickly, "You'll have to forgive Daddy for rambling, he has a touch of jet lag. Let me brief you. Faradeux Industries is a conglomerate involved in ranching, meat packing, and other related activities. Next month our stock is going to start trading on the New York Stock Exchange. A small organization here in New York City finds our involvement in food production to be..."

Her forehead wrinkled as she searched for the proper words. "They think our activities are morally offensive. We don't agree." She handed me the thick file. "This contains background information on our company and copies of the letters we have received from the group threatening to disrupt the ceremonies."

"What ceremonies?"

Jacob Faradeux proudly answered. "On the day we're listed, I'm going to ring the gong to open the trading at the Exchange. It's a special honor. I don't want any protestors ruining my day. I want you to find out what they're planning and stop them."

"That sounds rather ominous." My partner, Eileen—who also happens to be my sister, three years older than I—stood in the doorway. Jacob rose from his chair. She motioned him to keep his seat and strode into the room, apologizing for her tardiness. "I'm sorry I'm late. I had an unexpected court appearance. What have I missed?"

I flashed a nasty look that meant "Not good enough. You'll pay for this later" and introduced everyone. Eileen took a seat on my left. I slid the packet of materials to her and watched the slow-motion look of dismay spread across Jacob's face, bronzed and lined from sixty years under his beloved Texas sun.

The huge cowboy squirmed uncomfortably in the roomful of women. I almost laughed. I smiled in what I hoped was a sympathetic manner and said, "Don't worry, Jacob, we do have a few men working here."

"Red, I don't care who you hire as long as you get results. The FBI fellas at Federal Plaza didn't tell me you were women but they did tell me you were the best. Now why don't we all have another round of java and talk business?"

Eileen was quiet. She scanned the material in the folder while I refilled the coffee mugs and asked Faradeux, "Why did you contact the FBI?"

Jacob began to answer, but his daughter held up a hand. "Daddy, let me." Nanci started talking, her fingernails softly rubbing against the arm of her chair as she explained. "We receive letters from a lot of people. Some contain valid complaints, others are a little crazy. We answer every one, regardless of who sent it."

From the corner of my eye, I saw Eileen studying one of the pages. Nanci paused, not sure if she should continue.

"Go on. Eileen reads, I listen."

Nanci smiled. "One of the groups here in Manhattan, WARM—the Worldwide Animal Rights Movement—heard about our plans and wrote to us. They threatened to stop us if we came to New York. We went to the FBI to see if they could help."

Eileen handed me the letter and said, "Ms. Faradeux, this letter does not contain any harassing or threatening language."

I picked up the letter. Nanci paused, waiting for my complete attention. I quickly scanned the paper.

"We are speaking for an oppressed group that has no voice. On their behalf, we demand that you immediately stop the torture of innocent animals. Fueled by your greed, your cruel and wasteful system of producing food exploits nonhumans who cannot protest for themselves...." The letter rambled on, filling the page with outrage at Faradeux Industries. It ended with the caveat: "Don't waste an opportunity to bring justice to the world. Use your upcoming celebration to celebrate the creation of a compassionate world. Free your animal slaves!''

I carefully put the letter down on top of the file Nanci had given me and looked across the table. Nanci looked uncomfortable, Jacob looked impatient. I wondered how long he'd be able to keep his temper under control. "Eileen's right. These people don't like your company's practices but they aren't threatening you. You're overreacting.''

"The FBI told us the same thing. That's why we came to see you. We want you to investigate. Daddy's afraid they might ruin his day—''

Jacob exploded. "Damn agitators! I'm not overreacting. They're out to get me! You must stop them.'' Faradeux pounded his fist on the table. The coffee cups jumped half an inch and landed without losing a drop. "Animal rights! What about my rights? What about the rights of my shareholders? What about the rights of people who want to eat steak?''

I WAS ENJOYING a well-deserved cigarette in the quiet of my office when Eileen came into the room. She sat on the edge of my desk and looked at me, her brown eyes twinkling with suppressed hilarity. In perfect harmony, we shouted, "What about the rights of people who want to eat steak?'' and broke into raucous laughter.

"So.'' Eileen addressed a plant in the corner of the room; she couldn't look at me without giggling. "Are we going to make the world safe for steak lovers?''

"Yeah—'' I rubbed my forehead and temples, trying to massage away the headache creeping in behind my eyes. "We can use the business. We'll check that group out, it shouldn't take too long. I'll send Faradeux a report and a huge bill. That should make him happy." I chuckled. "When he pays, we'll go out for a steak dinner."

"Who at Federal Plaza sent this guy to us? Was it a friend or foe?"

It's amazing how fast a good day can turn sour. One minute you're smiling and joking, sixty seconds later it's gone bad. Suddenly you're not smiling anymore, you're searching for the aspirin bottle, wishing you had never climbed out of your safe bed. I stopped laughing and said, "Halstead."

"Oh." The word hung in the air. I didn't want to talk about Dennis Halstead. I picked up a pencil and idly sketched a group of interlocking circles.

Several years ago, Dennis and I had enjoyed a brief, but passionate, affair. The affair ended a few weeks after he introduced me to his close friend and colleague, Jeff Stewart. Jeff and I married six months after we met. Two weeks before our fourth anniversary, my husband was killed in a botched drug raid. I dove into a well of self-pity, fueled by nonstop drinking that lasted for years. All that happened four years ago—I've been sober for a year now and working hard to stay sober.

Halstead had made several attempts to revive the liaison. Convinced he was motivated more by pity than passion, I rebuffed his advances. Dennis eventually withdrew; I was never sure if he was disappointed or relieved.

Our infrequent meetings hummed with these undercurrents from our past. Now I'd have to call with thanks for sending me a beef-growing paranoid who

wanted me to be sure his party wasn't spoiled by people with a different point of view. The pencil point
snapped and I threw the pencil on the desk.

Eileen cleared her throat. "Blaine, I need you to do
a little favor for me. Your pal Tony Parker is hassling
one of my clients. I want you to find out why."

The day was hopelessly lost; the headache hit with
full force. I tore the page from the pad and tossed it
into the garbage can. "Who's the client?"

"Hurley Blake. You haven't met him." She took
one of my cigarettes and fumbled in her pocket for
matches.

I snapped my lighter, held the flame under the cigarette, and said, "Quit stalling. Is this another pro
bono case?"

"And you never take in strays."

Our penchant for getting involved in freebie cases
was a touchy subject. I had spent the weekend review-
ing our quarterly income statements and knew we had
to give more attention to clients who would actually
pay for our services. But I couldn't argue—I had taken
as much from our bottom line with volunteer work as
Eileen. And we went into business together to get away
from bosses who preached profit above all else. And
we had made a profit during each of the seven years
we had been in business together. And we were on
track to do it again this year....

I tossed the lighter on the desk and sighed. "Who's
Hurley Blake?"

Eileen smiled; apology accepted. "He owns a small
bodega on the Lower East Side. Hurley wasn't making any money when he opened the store so he diver-

sified. He spent five or six years operating as the local bookie."

Had my normally rational sister gone insane? I interrupted her. "Excuse me—when did we start representing bookies? Did I miss the meeting where we approved a change in corporate philosophy?"

"No change." Eileen laughed harshly. "We're still fighting for truth, justice, and the American way."

She wasn't joking. When we were setting up our business, a combination law and investigative firm, Eileen had semi-seriously suggested engraving the familiar Superman motto across the top of our letterhead. I mockingly countered with, "To the batpoles, Robin!" and our first stalemate ensued. Our letterhead was printed sans motto.

Eileen continued. "Hurley Blake dropped out of the business three or four years ago. He said it was because he was afraid he'd lose custody of his daughter. I think something else scared him out."

My head was throbbing, pounding away at my forbearance. For the second time that morning I muttered, "Get to the point."

"Hurley's clean but Parker keeps threatening to lock him up and put the girl in a foster home. I was late this morning because Parker did it again." Eileen used the glowing end of the cigarette to light another. I raised an eyebrow; chain-smoking was Eileen's signal for badly frayed nerves.

I held out an ashtray for the spent butt and said, "You're the attorney around here, why don't you file a complaint against Parker? Hit the city with a suit for twenty or thirty million dollars. If he is stepping over the line that should stop him."

Eileen scratched her head and exhaled. "My client refuses to let me take any action. He just calls each time Parker raids the shop, expecting me to fix things. But he won't give me straight answers. Parker won't talk to me either. You were close when you were on the force, maybe he'll talk to you. Will you call him?"

"Okay, I'll talk to him. Maybe I can get him to leave your client alone."

"Thanks." Eileen hopped off the desk and headed out of the office. She stopped at the doorway. "Let me know if I can help with Faradeux."

Peace and quiet descended on my office. I found some aspirin, washed the tablets down with the cold coffee left in my mug, and tried to concentrate on the work piled up on my desk. It was a futile attempt. I dialed the 49th Precinct and asked for the commander.

THE RIVERVIEW BAR & Grill may not be the best bar in the world, but even though I don't drink anymore it's still number one on my list. The RiverView, called "the View" by everyone in the neighborhood, never had a view of any river, but over the past fifty-seven years enough beer to fill the Hudson River has flowed through its shiny taps. The View has thick juicy hamburgers, friendly bartenders, and a jukebox filled with the latest music. Best of all, it's a corner tavern, twelve doors away from my own front door.

Some of the regulars complain about too many yuppie puppies taking up their space, but Bobby and Ryan, the owners/bartenders, have worked hard to keep the View a local haven. Both groups manage to coexist peacefully. They have to; six-foot-ten-inch

Bobby tosses out anyone who breaks the peace—no discussion allowed.

At quarter to five in the afternoon, not many members of either group were seeking haven. Only a few men were hunched over the bar, nursing their afternoon beers. I started to make myself comfortable on a bar stool but changed my mind. I grabbed the sweaty mug of seltzer and headed for the privacy of the rear booths. Bobby, who takes charge of the tables while Ryan handles the bar, keeps large Reserved signs on those booths, holding them for the exclusive use of View regulars.

I was a regular; Parker wasn't. He was sitting on a stool at the far end of the room, staring at the half inch of beer in his mug. I touched Tony on the shoulder and led him to the back of the saloon. Bobby delivered fresh drinks and disappeared, taking the opportunity to check out my guest. He nodded and winked at me; Parker was okay.

We spent half an hour catching up and gossiping about mutual acquaintances on the force. Years ago, when I was idealistic and fresh out of college, I spent sixteen months as one of New York's finest, hating every second of my tour. Parker became my self-appointed mentor.

I still remember the night I told Parker I was going to quit. We spent hours sitting at his kitchen table, drinking whiskey and arguing about my decision. I resigned the next morning.

Parker rose through the ranks. Now he was a captain with his own command, his lifelong ambition realized. But Tony didn't look happy with his achievement—he was tense and drawn. He quickly gulped his beer and impatiently waited for Bobby to bring refills.

"I haven't heard from you for months. What do you need? I know you didn't wake up this morning and think it would be a lovely day to have a few drinks with your old sarge."

Bobby brought another drink to the table and looked at my empty stein. I shook my head and waited for him to leave. Hoping Parker was mellowed by the beer, I took a deep breath and said, "Eileen mentioned that she saw you this morning. She told me you've been harassing one of our clients."

Tony slammed the mug down on the table. Sensing trouble, Bobby glided closer. I waved him away and said to Tony, "Eileen is ready to make an official complaint. I thought I'd talk to you first, see if we can work this out."

Speaking more to himself than me, Parker mumbled, "Hurley Blake."

"Yeah, Hurley Blake. What's going on?"

"Blake's a scumbag. Tell your sister to keep away from him."

"Eileen said you're pulling a lot of bogus stunts. That's not your style—you taught me to go by the book. Why don't you ease off this guy for a while?"

"Shit, you couldn't make it past rookie. Now you're giving me advice. Don't tell me how to run my precinct." He yanked a roll of cash from his pocket and tossed a twenty on the table. "Don't call me the next time you need a favor."

"Tony..." I tried to think of something that wouldn't cause another outburst. "I'm sorry. I wasn't trying to make you angry."

The apology caught Tony off guard—I don't often apologize. Tony blinked and tried to smile. He was out of practice, the muscles pulled his face to a grimace.

"Listen, kid, don't pay attention to me. Remember how we used to complain that the old man in charge didn't have a sense of humor?"

I nodded. "I remember. I also remember how you swore that would never happen to you."

"The good old days. We had all the answers." Tony shook his head and attempted another smile. "I shouldn't a yelled. I've been doing too much of that lately. Tell your sister I'll back off. You know your old sarge, always trying too hard to get the bad guys off the street. Tell Eileen I'm sorry." He laughed; I caught a glimpse of the carefree sergeant who used to keep me out of trouble. "Won't be the last time I get some smart lawyer mad at me."

"If that's an apology, we accept." I pointed at his empty beer mug and asked, "Do you want another?"

"Nope." Tony pushed the bill to the center of the table and stood up. "I gotta go, I'm already late for a meeting. This one's on me—next time you buy."

Bobby, who's never slow when there's money on the table, grabbed the bill before Parker was halfway to the door. Bobby glanced at the twenty, then looked at me. "You get about six more refills or I get a nice tip. Which is it?"

"You get the tip. I'm going home."

Bobby smiled and stuffed the money into the hip pocket of his tight, faded jeans. I slowly drank the rest of the seltzer and smoked a cigarette, trying to imagine the stress of running a precinct that was turning Parker into a humorless, prematurely old man.

The goodwill brought with the large tip evaporated as the evening crowd floated in. Bobby started to hover around the booth, impatient to turn it over to a paying customer. My seltzer was gone. I didn't feel like drinking another glass of seltzer or smoking another cigarette; there wasn't any reason to hang around. So I went home and stayed there long enough to call Eileen for Hurley Blake's address. I traded my skirt for jeans, my heels for sneakers, and went out to visit Blake's store on Avenue B.

AS YOU WALK EAST on St. Mark's Place, Greenwich Village's charming eccentricity fades. It disappears entirely when you cross First Avenue to Avenue A and enter a new world known as Alphabet City. Poverty, crumbling housing, the highest crime rate in the city, and every type of drug imaginable are woven together in the blocks between avenues A and D. Most tourists and people who live in other parts of the city never knowingly venture into the neighborhood, with good reason.

I walked around Tompkins Square Park—even the cops are afraid to walk *through* the park—to Avenue B. Halfway down the block, smoke drifted past my nose. I sprinted around the corner and saw a teenage girl pulling open the door of a burning building. Smoke whirled out through the narrow crack and flames ignited the boxes of rice and pasta displayed in the window of the grocery store—the store Hurley Blake owned.

"Don't!" I grabbed the collar of the girl's jacket and pulled her back. "You can't go in there. You'll get yourself killed."

"Fuck you! My daddy's inside!" she screamed. "Let me go! I have to get him out!"

The girl struggled to break fee. Her flailing arms connected with the side of my head, and a sharp kick landed on my shin. The unexpected combination knocked me off balance; she squirmed away from me and scrambled to the entrance. I regained my footing and wrapped my arms around the girl's waist before she reached the door. Her fists lashed out, searching for my head. I ducked, grabbed her wrists, and spun her around against a parked car. Terrified brown eyes focused on my face.

I yelled, "Are you sure there's somebody inside?"

"My daddy—it's his store. Let go of me!"

The girl tried to shake her wrists loose; panic added to her strength. I tightened my grasp and shouted, "There's a firebox around the corner. Go pull the alarm!"

Her feet stuck to the cement, paralyzed by fear. I yanked the girl off the car and slapped her on the back, pushing her in the direction of the alarm. "Move, damn it—I'll get your dad." With stumbling feet, she started down the street, looking back over her shoulder as she ran. I took a deep breath and pulled the door open.

The stream of fresh air briefly parted the thick smoke. I saw a few rows of shelves filled with groceries, some of the packages already in flames. The edges of the dark cloud welded together and a rush of hot air hit my face, scorching my throat and lungs. I dropped to my hands and knees to breathe the cooler air near the floor and crawled to the check-out counter.

A line of boxes above my head burst into flames and exploded, showering me with bits of cereal and burning cardboard. I shook them from my hair and peered behind the counter. The space was empty.

The wall of fire edged closer. It jumped across a narrow aisle and wrapped around a second row of shelves. The layer of dense smoke pressed closer to the floor, heating the breathable air. Panic built in my oxygen-starved lungs. I coughed uncontrollably and squinted to clear my smoke-filled eyes. A chunk of ceiling tile flamed and dropped to the floor. Little tongues of fire shot out in all directions.

Decision time. I could still find my way to the door and safety. No one would blame me for abandoning the search—no one except the terror-stricken girl waiting outside. I wiped soot from my eyes and crawled to the rear of the store.

Fluorescent lights exploded, coating the floor with razor-sharp bits of white glass. Popcorn started to pop. Jars of baby food, spaghetti sauce, and other condiments burst, throwing glass and hot liquid at me. The rumbling flames mixed with the sounds of breaking glass, blending together into an overwhelming roar of destruction.

The dense smoke hovered inches above the floor, reducing the visibility until I couldn't see beyond the length of my arm. The wall of flames hurdled overhead and fell on the last length of shelves, sending another deluge of glass and glowing embers to the floor. Decision made: It was time to get the hell out of the inferno.

I turned, and my feet brushed against a bundle. I groped in the smoky darkness; my fingers touched a man's soft cotton T-shirt. I pressed my fingers against the artery in his throat and felt a feeble pulse. Praying that I had found Hurley Blake, I wrapped my arm around his chest and pulled. He was as heavy and responsive as a sack of cement.

Drag, cough, gasp for air, rest. We made slow progress. I stopped thinking, stopped trying to brush off the burning embers falling on me, and concentrated on the pattern.

Drag, cough, gasp for air, rest. We moved one slow foot at a time.

Drag. Cough. Gasp for air. Rest.

The pungent smoke extended itself to the floor and I was lost. Disoriented by the flames and smoke, I collapsed and rested my head on the floor, trying to catch my breath. Too exhausted to move. Breaths away from giving up to the smoke. I closed my eyes. The hot tiles burned my cheek.

Hurley stirred under my arm, silently urging me on. I tightened my hold on him and blindly crept forward, plowing through the ashes drifting down from the ceiling.

A glowing hunk of wood landed on my arm. I shook it off and moved ahead into a wall. The wall moved. A trace of clean air wafted past my nose.

The door? I pushed my shoulder against it and tumbled out onto the sidewalk, dragging the heavy body behind. Someone pried my fingers away from his shirt and covered my face with a mask. I clutched it with both hands and greedily inhaled the sweet oxygen.

"YOU WERE LUCKY—once again." Dr. Mabe cut a piece of adhesive and tossed the roll of tape on a tray next to the bed. I didn't feel lucky. My entire body ached, my throat and lungs burned every time I inhaled. I wanted to pull the covers over my head and sleep for a week.

I croaked, "When can I go home?" The harsh sound of my voice surprised me.

"Not until I'm sure you're okay." The doctor pressed a gauze pad over the burn on my forearm and gently taped it down. "You inhaled a lot of smoke and soot. I want to be sure everything's working the way it should before I let you out of my sight."

I sat up on the edge of the guerney and stared at my bare feet; I wanted to take a shower. Dr. Mabe kicked the pile of rags on the floor. "Your clothes stink. No cabbie's going to pick you up if you're wearing them. I called your sister."

"You called Eileen?"

Dr. Mabe laughed. "Part of Saint Katherine's special services for frequent patients. Eileen's on her way. She's going to bring replacement clothing." She finished taping the bandage then stepped back to look at me. "How long have I known you? Three, four years? I'm getting tired of patching you up."

"Don't lecture, I pay my bills." I yawned. "Don't you have any other patients to bother?"

"Nope." Dr. Mabe was too cheerful for someone in charge of a Manhattan emergency room. "Business is always slow on Monday night. People are recovering from the weekend. They stay home and don't get hurt. I don't know what we would have done for excitement if you hadn't come around." The stethoscope slipped from its perch around her neck. She jammed it into the pocket of her lab jacket and sat next to me. "What happened this time? I didn't get the complete story when the paramedics brought you in."

We were interrupted before I had to answer. A nurse walked into the room and apologized for the intrusion. He handed her a chart and said, "Dr. Rabin is looking for you."

My doctor sighed and absentmindedly ran a hand through her hair as she read the chart, exposing hidden gray strands. The short, dark hair obediently fell back into place as soon as she removed her hand. She closed the chart and slid to her feet, saying, "Be right back."

I stopped her. "Dr. Mabe—would you find out how Hurley Blake is doing?" She didn't recognize the name. I said, "The guy I pulled from the building, could you find out how he is?"

"Sure, I'll look in on him." She looked at me and ordered: "Just lie down and take it easy. Don't go anywhere until I get back."

Don't go anywhere—what a joke. I followed the doctor's advice and rested my head on the pillows. When I closed my eyes a vivid image of burning walls instantly appeared. A faint odor of smoke drifted past my face, mixing reality with fantasy until I wasn't sure if I was back in the fire or safely out of its reach.

I sat up, expecting to see flames, and laughed at my unsteady nerves. Dr. Mabe was right; my clothes did stink. I got to my feet, and kicked the bundle of rags into the corner next to the trash can. Let the janitors deal with the stinking mess. I fell back on the guerney, pressed my eyes closed again, and tried to relax.

Dr. Mabe re-entered the room. She misinterpreted my closed eyes and started to back out quietly. Eager for the companionship, I sat up and said, "I'm awake."

"It may be a mistake to release you. Just say the word, I'll have you upstairs and tucked into bed without any delay."

"No, thanks." With a show of energy I didn't have, I sat up on the edge of the cot and swung my feet to the floor. "I'd rather sleep in my own bed. Can I leave?"

She nodded. "The lab tests look good. I don't see any reason to keep you. Eileen's waiting outside." She handed me a pill bottle and a bag. "Here's something to help you sleep and some clean clothes. Go home and go to bed. I want to see you tomorrow before you do anything else."

A chilling shriek pierced the closed door. Afraid of the answer I would receive, I whispered, "What was that?"

"Hurley Blake's daughter. He died without regaining consciousness. I'm sorry." Dr. Mabe put her hand on my shoulder and said, "You did what you could. Go home."

There wasn't much to say after that. Eileen took charge of the details and before my numb brain thawed enough to think, we were home. I dragged myself up the stairs to the bathroom. Eileen, my guardian angel, hovered behind.

"What are you doing?"

"Taking a bath. I can't stand the smell." I turned on the water taps. "What are *you* doing?"

"Worrying." She sat on the counter and watched me adjust the water and add the soap powder.

"Great." I stripped, shut the water off, and gingerly eased into the bath. I carefully arranged my left arm on the edge of the tub so the bandage wouldn't get wet and said, "You're good at worrying. You probably don't need my help."

"I talked with..."

I wasn't listening. I was remembering Hurley's feeble movement and the way it had encouraged me to keep crawling out of the store. I swatted a clump of soap suds against the wall. The foam stuck to the blue tiles and quivered once before slipping down to the water. "I can't believe he died. What if I had gotten there a few minutes earlier?"

"Don't be stupid." Eileen tossed a washcloth at my head. I batted the cloth down into the tub and rested my head against the cool tiles. "You did all you could. Don't play 'What if?' You'll make yourself crazy. Take a lesson from the Greeks—blame the Fates."

"Ahh, the Greeks. What are you talking about?"

Eileen had discovered Greek mythology when she was twelve years old. Bored by books like *Little Women*, she sneaked a book of Greek fables past the ill-humored librarian who thought little girls shouldn't be filling their heads with such nonsense, and was hooked for life.

She eagerly explained. "Life is a thread; the Fates control it. Clotho, the first Fate, spins the thread of life. Lachesis determines the length of the thread. Atropos, the third Fate, holds the scissors. When she snips, it's all over. Blame Atropos, not yourself."

The pills were beginning to work; I was too sleepy to argue. I grunted and climbed out of the tub. Eileen handed me a towel and followed me to my bedroom. Yawning, I dried myself and tumbled into bed, barely able to stay awake long enough to say good-night. "Thanks for coming to my rescue. Lock up on your way out. I'll see you in the morning."

"I'm going to stay here tonight. You shouldn't be alone; I'd worry about you all night if I went home."

"Suit yourself." I pulled the sheet up to my ears and mumbled, "Make yourself comfortable. You know where everything is."

Despite Eileen's advice to blame the Fates, "What if?" climbed into bed beside me. Whenever I drifted close to sleep, the faint smell of smoke coming from my hair set off the whispering voice. What if? Would Hurley Blake still be alive?

Seeking diversion, I turned the bedside radio on. Nanci Griffith's soft voice mocked me—"If wishes were changes we'd all live in roses and there wouldn't be children who cried in their sleep." I fell asleep wondering if Wina Blake was crying in her sleep.

TWO

THE MORNING WAS almost over by the time I forced myself from the bed. Eileen was long gone, having left behind a note taped to the coffeemaker. "Go see Dr. Mabe before you come to the office. Better yet, take the day off. We'll try to survive without you."

I thought about following her advice but didn't. A long shower, bandaged arm carefully wrapped in plastic, and a strong cup of coffee made me ready to face what was left of the day. My visit to the hospital was brief. Dr. Mabe pronounced me fit and warned me to keep away from cigarettes and burning buildings for at least a week. More good advice that I promised to think about.

The doctor's lecture didn't include warnings about buildings that were no longer burning: I went back to Hurley Blake's store to examine the ruins. The subway left me at Astor Place, from which I walked into the decaying Lower East Side. In the harsh daylight, it's impossible to ignore the blight or believe the political promises of a rebirth. I quickly moved past the abandoned tenements and kept a watchful eye on the street life.

A man, his age camouflaged by dirt and dried vomit smeared across his face, squatted in front of a dilapidated café crying, "They stole my dentures. They stole my dentures."

How do you comfort someone who's had his teeth stolen? His companions offered sympathy by passing a bottle and gently patting his shoulder. I shook my head and kept walking.

The bodega's shattered door and windows had been covered with large sheets of plywood. Looters, searching for God knows what, had already torn most of the wood away from the door. Grateful that my shaky muscles wouldn't be called upon to gain access, I ducked under the hanging boards and went to the back of the store.

I sniffed the calm, smoky air and remembered the scolding delivered the night before by one of the firemen. "You should never run into a burning building. It's a sure way to get killed." The realization of just how lucky I had been sent tremors of fear across my back. I shook them off and kicked aside the debris blocking the aisle.

The rubble brought to mind pictures of the destruction left behind by World War II bombers. Pieces of broken glass, charred wood, and puddles of black water were scattered across the floor. Tiny particles of ash hung in the air, disturbed by my presence.

I sniffed the air. Smoke. Burned groceries. Something else I couldn't identify. The odors prompted memories of the fire. Closing my eyes, I replayed the scene in slow motion.

Even in slow motion, the rapid acceleration of the fire surprised me. I took another deep breath. My surprise turned to suspicion: a rapidly spreading fire, a strange odor that reminded me of gunpowder. Signs of arson.

I opened my eyes and carefully looked around. The frozen food cases lining the rear wall of the store had been blown apart; the gap was wide enough for a person to step through to the storeroom on the other side. The linoleum floor around the cases was shredded and torn, exposing a foot-wide circle of bare concrete. Hurley Blake's store hadn't been burned down, it had been blown down.

I stepped into the shallow crater. One of the many nails strewn across the floor punctured the sole of my right sneaker and slid into the empty space between my toes. I was trying to dig it out, breaking a fingernail in the attempt, when I heard light footsteps inadvertently crunch a bit of glass. I turned. Hurley Blake's daughter was walking down the aisle, a snub-nosed .38 Special rigidly held out in front of her body.

Five shots. Accuracy wouldn't be a problem—you don't have to be a marksman when you're five feet away from your target.

"Hey, take it easy. Put the gun down, I'm not going to hurt you." I held my hands out in a nonthreatening gesture and took a step toward her.

"Don't move, bitch."

"Okay." I stopped and set my feet a shoulder's width apart, the right foot about twelve inches ahead of its mate, and calmly repeated, "Take it easy."

"Shut up." The girl walked closer and snarled, "Shut up, or I'll blow your fucking head off your fucking shoulders."

One more step and she would be close enough to grab. I rocked forward onto the balls of my feet and smiled. My failure to respond angered the stocky teenager; she prodded my chest with the stubby gun barrel.

"What's the matter, bitch? You scared? You should be. You trying to rip us off?"

"I'm not trying to rip you off. I pulled your father out of the fire last night."

"You want me to thank you? Well, I'm not thanking anybody. He died." Unshed tears magnified her dark eyes.

The young girl wiped her eyes with the back of her free hand. I lunged, put my thumbs on the back of her gun hand, and bent it back to a neat right angle. The girl struggled to break loose. I hate to beat up on kids, but I'd also hate to be shot by one—I increased the pressure. She whimpered a foul curse and dropped the revolver.

I held the wristlock with one hand and crouched to grab the gun with the other. Once it was in my pocket, safely out of her reach, I dropped her hand and said, "You must be Edwina Blake."

"Name's Wina." Sullenly kneading her wrist, she mumbled, "Gimme back my gun."

"So you can shoot me?" I laughed. "No, I think I'll hang on to it for a while. What are you doing with a gun?"

"Friends told me people were busting in here, stealing stuff. I was gonna stop them." She kicked a piece of charred wood into a puddle and looked around. "Ain't much left to steal. What do you want?"

I couldn't explain to those angry eyes the feeling of her father moving beneath my arms and how that memory drew me back. I shrugged. "I work with your father's attorney. I came here last night to talk about the trouble he was having with the police."

"Too late. He don't need your help now." Wina kicked another chunk of wood across the floor. "I don't need it either. Get the fuck out of here."

I lost my temper. "You need somebody's help. Look around. See how those cases are blown apart? Fires don't do that. This wasn't an accident." I handed her a business card. "They always know where to reach me. Call if you need anything."

Wina took the card and snapped her fingers against it. "What kind of help can you give me?"

"I don't know." I was regretting the impulsive action; picking up strays can be painful. The first lame thing that came to my mouth popped out. "Maybe you need a quiet place to study." I shrugged. "You decide."

Wina Blake wasn't impressed. She popped her fingers against the card again. "Only help you can give is to give my gun back."

I shook my head. "Sorry. No gun."

She dropped the card from lifeless fingers. It fluttered to the floor. Wina used the toe of her black hightops to slowly grind the card into the ash-covered tiles. "I'll get another gun. I'm gonna find the motherfucker who killed my daddy and kill him."

"This isn't something you should get involved in—"

"Fuck you!" The girl turned and ran from the store.

I pulled the nail from my shoe and dropped it in my pocket on top of the gun. Then I wasted another ten or fifteen minutes kicking the wreckage and peering into boxes before giving up. I rearranged the plywood blockade and walked out to St. Mark's Place to stop a cab.

I STROLLED into the workroom for a cup of coffee and smiled. Word processors were quietly spitting out documents, telephones were ringing; my staff was hard at work. I hoped they were earning enough to cover my charity work.

Eileen wasn't in her office so I headed for my own and groaned when I saw my desk. Overnight, the stack of files piled on top had grown by half a foot. I stared warily at the folders and wondered if the ache in my shoulders was leftover fatigue or an excuse to avoid the work I didn't want to do.

Eileen appeared to interrupt the debate. "Hi. Marcella told me you were in." Marcella, our receptionist, carefully tracks all arrivals and departures. "I was starting to worry about you. Every time I called your house, I got your stupid answering machine. How do you feel?"

"I'm fine. There isn't anything for you to worry about." I waved my hand over the files. "Do you ever worry that we've gotten too successful? Too much paperwork. Not enough field work."

Eileen laughed and sat down. "Yesterday you were complaining about a lack of business, today we have too much. I was going to ask who you're going to assign to the Faradeux case but I guess you've decided to handle it yourself."

"No reason not to do it myself. I'm bored. Dr. Mabe said it was okay—as long as I keep out of fires."

Eileen laughed again. "Please, take the case. You've been pretty grouchy lately. We'll all be happier when you get out of this office and do some real work. How are you going to approach WARM?"

I smiled. "I've already approached them. I called their office and dropped a few hints that I might make a donation. They are holding a seminar tonight. I'll go listen to their pitch. I might even become a convert and ban all hamburgers from the office."

"You'll have a mutiny on your hands. And don't ask me to defend you, I'll be on their side."

I laughed and leaned back in my chair; my arm brushed against the metal lump in my pocket. I stopped laughing, dug the gun out, and tossed it on the desk. "It isn't loaded. The shells are in my other pocket. I met Hurley Blake's daughter a little while ago. Wina's a charming girl with a very limited vocabulary. She threatened to blow my fucking head off—that's her adjective, not mine. I thought it best to disarm her."

Eileen picked the gun up and wrinkled her nose in distaste. "It's too easy for people to get hold of these things." She cautiously put the revolver back on the desk and asked, "Where did you run into her?"

"We met at the store. When I went back to the hospital this morning for my checkup, Dr. Mabe said something that made me curious. She said Hurley Blake died from internal injuries and severe bleeding, not the smoke inhalation or burns you would expect from a fire. So, I went back to the store for a look around. It looks as if a bomb exploded in there. I'm going to call Tony and see what the cops and fire department think."

Something else was bothering me—my conscience. I rubbed the base of my neck and felt a knot of tension growing under my fingers. "I made a huge mistake and told Wina Blake that I thought the fire had been set. She stomped out, promising to kill the person responsible." I swept the revolver into a desk drawer and locked it. "The kid's crazy enough to try." I silently added, *I have to stop her.* "Tell me about Hurley Blake."

Eileen lit a cigarette, took a drag, and blew the smoke at the ceiling. I watched enviously. I wanted a cigarette, but remembered Dr. Mabe's advice, and played with the tiny nail instead.

"Hurley was forty years old. He doesn't have any other children. I don't know anything about his wife. They lived on Eighth Street with his mother. Legal Aid referred him to me—I've been picking up some of their overflow cases. I don't know anything else about the man."

Eileen's visit evolved into a general business discussion. Most people don't understand how two sisters can work together, and enjoy it, but it's impossible for me to imagine any other arrangement.

We tried working for other people and hated it. I even tried working alone and really hated it. After seven years together, our partnership has achieved a stable, mature level—we scream at each other only once or twice a month. Our screaming sessions are always held in the privacy of the conference room, safely away from inquisitive staff ears. When we finish yelling at each other, it's business as usual.

The rest of the day faded away peacefully. I made several calls to Tony Parker, which were never returned, and managed to work on—or give away—the files on my desk. I was down to the last half dozen when Eileen walked past the open door and called, "Good night!"

Whenever my workaholic sister leaves, it's time to go home. I yelled for her to wait and hurried out, leaving papers scattered across the top of my desk. Eileen looked at my clothes and snickered. "You look ready to protest. Where's the meeting—McDonald's?"

"Right, the Burger King is the keynote speaker."

She missed the sarcasm and began to hum the jingle from one of the hamburger chains' commercials. I snapped, "Stop it." Eileen raised her eyebrows and stopped humming.

Stage fright. Opening night jitters. I was jumpy, which isn't unusual. I'm always nervous before starting any undercover operation. Once I settle into the role, I'm fine, but I can't joke before I start. Jacob Faradeux was a clown but he was my clown; I wouldn't make the mistake of underestimating his opponents. Extremists, regardless of their cause, make me nervous.

The elevator touched down in the lobby. We walked out and Eileen delivered her usual caution. "Please be careful. Don't be stupid." As always, I promised to obey.

ONCE OWNED by Clement Moore, the author of "A Visit from St. Nicholas," Chelsea is crammed into the thirty blocks between the Garment District and the Village. Former home of Dylan Thomas, Andy Warhol, Jack Kerouac, Mark Twain, and Sid Vicious,

Chelsea is being overrun by the discount stores and office condos that are homogenizing the rest of the island.

The people at WARM didn't waste their money on fancy office space. The building, an unkempt orphan in the center of a group of well-groomed brownstones, had been skipped by the rebuilding mania engulfing the block.

The outside was chipped and crumbling, the inside worse. The lobby was decorated in 3-D: dirt, dark, and dank. I punched the elevator button and waited. The elevator never arrived. I found the staircase and ran up six flights, arriving at the top barely winded and pleased—no lingering effects from the previous night's excursion.

A man, handsome enough to rival any of the reigning heartthrobs, greeted me at the door. Dark tan, blue eyes, lopsided grin. I stared. My well-trained eyes detected a muscular chest hidden under a plain work shirt. A few dark hairs curled out from beneath the open collar.

"Those stairs are killers. Come in and sit down before you pass out. My name's Grant Wilder. I'm the doorman tonight." He shook my hand; the last two fingers on his right hand were missing. He muttered, "Vietnam."

I dragged my eyes away from those curly hairs and managed to introduce myself. "I'm Blaine Stewart. I called earlier today—I think I spoke to you."

Grant's forehead wrinkled. I could see the thought "Donor—be careful" go through his mind. He said casually, "Oh yes. I remember the name. I'm glad you were able to get here."

An elderly couple hesitated on the doorstep. Grant's eyes darted away to look at them, then came back to me. "Those folks look a little lost. I'm the official greeter so I better go do my job before they run away. Wait for me after the program. I'll tell you more about our organization."

I promised to wait. Grant rewarded me with a brilliant smile and gently squeezed my hand before releasing it. I took an aisle seat in the last row and watched him greet the newcomers.

Wilder worked the crowd with the skill of a politician, shaking hands and talking, seemingly unaware of his charismatic appeal. It was a good act, but the bursts of charm lasted a moment too long; the smile was a little too brilliant. I didn't believe Grant was oblivious to its effect.

Thirty people eventually filled the room and tried to make themselves comfortable on the metal chairs. Thirty-one, if my numb butt was added to the count. It was seven forty-nine, long past the meeting's starting time. I impatiently glanced over my shoulder and witnessed the passionate end of a discussion between Grant and a petite, dark-haired woman.

After an extended kiss, she broke away and hurried to the front of the room. Grant took a seat across the aisle from me, caught my eye, and shrugged as if to say, It happens all the time. He crossed his legs and casually studied the audience.

Slightly more women than men. Sixties hippies searching for a new cause, earnest young preppies, an elderly silver-haired couple, a six pack of matrons, and a handful of college students. No one looked like a lunatic, but how can you tell? These days lunatics come dressed in pin-striped suits, carrying American Express cards and cellular phones hidden in expensive briefcases.

The woman waited for the noise to settle and introduced herself as Rosalynn Carter. "No relation to Jimmy." The row of maturescent women giggled softly. Rosalynn nodded to acknowledge them and started her talk. Every word was written on large index cards. She read to us in a wispy monotone, not once daring to lift her gaze; the audience was drifting away on waves of ennui. I tried to listen but my mind kept wandering back to my encounter with Wina Blake.

"Faradeux" penetrated my reverie. I turned my attention back to Rosalynn's speech. ". . . a horrible example of the brutality practiced by the flesh-raising and slaughter industry which obscures its savageness under the description of meat production. Meat production is a polite, sanitized term for murder."

Indignation strengthened Rosalynn's voice. "When we purchase these products, we are purchasing dead flesh. The dead flesh of oppressed animals who have been abused and tortured. The video you are about to watch depicts the short, painful life of cattle raised and killed by Faradeux Industries. The filming took place on various Faradeux properties. It's real—nothing was staged for the camera."

Rosalynn wheeled a television monitor to the front and turned it on. Grant dimmed the overhead lights. The video was an amateur production, filmed with one of the new hand-held cameras that allow anyone to create his or her personal cinema verité.

The film opened with a shot of a large sign suspended over a dirt road. The sign proudly proclaimed the land to be under the ownership of Faradeux Industries. The lens leisurely opened to a wide-angle view of young cattle peacefully grazing in a field. The pastoral scene abruptly disappeared, replaced by a kaleidoscope of red-hot brands being applied to the animals. Tiny puffs of smoke rose from the singed hides.

Rosalynn wisely let the vivid images speak to our imaginations. Cattle were loaded on a truck, which the camera followed on a long journey to a feedlot in Colorado. Thinner, weak animals stumbled down the ramp into a fenced-in dirt ring occupied by hundreds of other steers. As the disoriented cattle struggled to maintain their balance on the steel ramp, I wondered if they could possibly be suffering from motion sickness. The action sped up, showing horns being removed and graphic castration scenes. My stomach rolled.

The camera didn't flinch as it followed the unsuspecting cattle into the slaughterhouse. They moved in a nervous, jerky line and were swept off their feet, suspended by an overhead conveyer belt so each dead animal wouldn't fall into the blood of its slaughtered predecessor. The lens froze on a bloody carcass and faded to black.

The lights returned to full strength. Rosalynn started to talk, rambling about the number of cattle crammed into the feedlots, the chemicals used to accelerate weight gain, and a thousand dry statistics. I rocked my chair back onto its hind legs to stretch my overly long legs, lulled into complacency by her hypnotic voice.

"Jacob Faradeux engineers the slaughter of hundreds of thousands of defenseless cattle with the same lack of humanity shown by Hitler to the Jews. He, like Hitler, must be stopped...."

Heads nodded in agreement. Outraged that no one objected to her trifling the Holocaust by comparing it to the production of hamburger meat, I let the chair's front legs crash to the floor and yelled, "How can you—"

Realizing I was about to blow my cover, I paused to rephrase my interruption. "How can we stop them? Faradeux controls a large, powerful organization."

Grant flashed me a "Good question" smile. Rosalynn did the same. "In a few weeks, Faradeux Industries will be listed for trading on the New York Stock Exchange. Honoring this corporation is a moral outrage. People who are concerned with ending oppression must rise up and protest. This meeting is a call to arms. We must mobilize to protest the existence of Faradeux Industries and demand the dissolution of their killing fields."

Enthusiastic applause muffled the rest of Rosalynn's answer. Another meeting was announced and refreshments were served. The pallid vegetables on the refreshment table didn't appeal to me. I walked past them and poured a cup of coffee. Grant Wilder appeared at my side as promised. He grabbed a handful of carrot sticks and flashed another smile at me. "What do you think?"

"That film was awesome. An impressive introduction to your work. Tell me more about your organization."

"It's not my organization." He took a noisy bite of a carrot stick and chewed. "Roz runs the show. I just assist. How did you hear about us?"

"The *Voice*."

"That was a good article." The *Village Voice*, the last of the city's muckraking papers, recently highlighted activist groups, mentioning WARM in one of the sidebars. The article had saved me a lot of research time; after I'd read it, I'd gratefully renewed my subscription.

Now I nodded to Grant in agreement. "It sure was. That article saved me a lot of time and trouble."

Grant raised an attractive eyebrow and asked, "How so?"

"One of my New Year's resolutions was to finally get involved with a group that was actually doing something about animal rights."

The eyebrows dipped then raised again. "The year's almost halfway gone. Your resolution didn't have much urgency behind it."

I sighed. "It's not that easy. When you're looking to donate time and money you have to be careful. There are too many groups who are willing to take my money. There aren't any who are able to show what they're doing to improve animal welfare. I hope WARM is different."

Grant brushed aside the hint of money as if it didn't matter and asked, "What other groups did you visit?"

"I'd rather not say. I don't like to say bad things about people I met only once or twice."

"As a jewel of gold in a swine's snout, so is a fair woman which is without discretion." He smiled.

"Proverbs. What can I tell you about our little group?"

We talked. Grant was a master at smoothly interrogating people, encouraging them to talk without realizing their answers were being stored for later scrutiny. He chewed on carrot sticks and pried. I gave evasive answers which seemed open and honest, and occasionally I alluded to searching for a worthy charity. My innocent smile smoothed the awkward moments.

I countered each question with one of my own. Wilder deftly turned my queries aside and came back with other questions. Somewhere between discussing antiwar protests and ignoring a question about where I lived, I passed some private test.

Grant finished eating his carrots and watched me refill my coffee cup. When I rejoined him at our spot near the front of the room, he said, "You're cautious and you've been around. I like that. We could use you. I'd like you to sit in on our next Executive Committee meeting. We need some new blood."

"Doesn't Rosalynn have to approve?"

"Don't worry about Roz. She listens to me. The meeting's here tomorrow night at seven-thirty. Can you make it?"

"Sure, I can clear my schedule." I smiled, delighted to have made such rapid progress.

The crowd slowly evaporated, leaving behind a few stragglers who drank the last of the coffee and scrounged through the limp remains of the vegetable platter. The elderly couple cornered Roz and Grant in the front of the room. I decided to leave before I found myself trapped with two inquisitive people focusing their suspicious attention on me. I waved good-bye to Grant. He called my name; I made believe I didn't hear him and walked out before he could get away.

My home is in Greenwich Village, fifteen or twenty blocks south of WARM's office. On a normal night, I would have walked home, enjoying the soft evening air, but not this time. I was worried about being followed—worried enough to take the subway.

The twenty-minute trip from Chelsea to my house stretched to forty-five minutes as I jumped from train to train, looking over my shoulder. Wasted time. Paranoid time.

Tired and annoyed, I dragged myself up the subway stairs and walked to Barrow Street. The dark windows of my empty house warned of the suffocating loneliness I'd find inside. I hurried past the house and walked until two in the morning, until exhaustion made me crave sleep more than companionship.

The light on the answering machine in the hallway was blinking, demanding I listen to its messages. I ignored it and stumbled up the stairs. Somehow, I managed to strip off my clothes before falling on the bed.

THREE

NIGHTMARES RUINED my sleep. Cowboys on immense black horses galloped in tightening circles, forcing me beneath a rusty hook dangling in the center of the field. The horses' sharp hooves cut into the dry ground, throwing clouds of dust into the air that momentarily blinded the riders.

I rolled under a split-rail fence into a grassy enclosure filled with cattle. They continued to graze peacefully, undisturbed by the blood gushing from deep gashes in their throats. Puddles of gore stained the stubby grass. I stepped in one and gagged. The harsh sound alerted the bloody steers; they lifted their heads and charged.

I tossed and turned to escape, pulled blankets over my head, and seconds later kicked them off. The red numbers of the digital clock flipped to 5:57. It was impossible to maintain the pretense of sleeping. I gave up and dressed in running clothes.

I smoke too many cigarettes, stay up too late, and never remember to take my vitamins. I try to atone for the abuse of my body by running, swimming, and walking fifteen or twenty hard miles each week—it's one of the few schedules I manage to follow.

Running is usually the most favorite part of my maintenance program, but not when I'm shaking off the hangover left behind by a sleepless night. I shuffled along the quiet predawn streets, sweating, wait-

ing for the euphoric moment when the knots in my
chest and legs would loosen. The runner's high never
arrived so I tried lying—Sure, I can finish two more
miles—cursing, and promising I'd never smoke, or
run, again. Even though I use them every time I run,
the promises always work. I finished my circuit without resorting to crawling and arrived back on my
block, virtuous and looking forward to breakfast.

Ida Yankovitch, the elderly woman who lived directly across the street, was out tending her flower
boxes. Ida was a member of the generation that didn't
believe in sleeping late. She watched my progress down
the street and waved when I ran into hailing distance.
I returned her greeting and bounced up the steps. Ida
scooted across the street and stood at the foot of the
stoop before I finished unlocking the door.

"Blaine, dear, I left a message on your answering
machine yesterday. Did you get it? Call me old-
fashioned, but I hate talking to those things. Modern
conveniences—modern *inconveniences,* if you ask me.
Who would have imagined we'd be so busy that we'd
need machines to answer the telephone? Don't get me
wrong, dear, I know you need one. You're always so
busy, I don't know how I'd ever get in touch with you
if you didn't have that little machine."

I often ran errands for her. You see, Ida never ven-
tured beyond the end of the block: two muggings
convinced her to stay close to home. The first rob-
bery was routine. Ida surrendered her purse, reported
the crime to the police, changed the locks on her
doors, and replaced the stolen items. Mugger number
two took her wallet and beat her for not carrying
enough money. I visited Ida in the hospital and

clutched her shaky hand as she cried and told me of
the attack. I remember silently vowing, If I ever catch
the bastard . . .

No one ever caught the bastard. After a few days in
the hospital, Ida was discharged. She went home and
changed the locks again. Three additional locks were
added and neighbors vowed to keep watchful eyes on
her, but Ida didn't believe them. She never walked
farther than the end of Barrow Street again.

Ida droned on about answering machines and the
end of civilization. I politely interrupted. "Ida, I'm
sorry. I didn't get home until late and didn't listen to
my messages." Sweat rolled down my forehead into
my eyes. Longing for a shower, I wiped it away and
asked, "Do you need something?"

"If it's not too much trouble, dear, I need something from the pet shop. Do you know, they won't
deliver to me anymore? The clerk—he was so rude—
told me it wasn't worth sending someone out for an
order under twenty-five dollars. These stores used to
do anything for their customers, now they just don't
care."

I wanted a shower, coffee, and breakfast. I didn't
want to be standing on the stoop, listening to my
neighbor's complaints about modern life. I had
enough trouble with my own life; I didn't really want
to listen to her. But I couldn't rudely send her away—
Ida reminded me of my own mother, happily putting
her life away on a golf course in Arizona. I wiped my
forehead again, rested against the wrought-iron railing, and patiently asked, "What do you need?"

"Mikey's eaten all his food and that darn bird won't
eat anything but the special mix from that store on

Broadway. I don't want you to go to any trouble, but we can't let him starve, can we?"

"No, Ida, we can't let him starve. Can Mikey hold out until this evening?" Mikey, a parakeet almost as old as Ida, couldn't skip many meals. "Or is he about to faint from hunger and fall off his perch?"

Ida giggled. She patted my arm and tried to reassure me. "Oh, dear, you're so funny. Of course Mikey can wait until tonight. I don't want you to go to any trouble, you do so much for me." Ida patted my arm again and excused herself to go back to her gardening.

I watched Ida hurry across the street and wondered how much energy I'd have at seventy-seven. I yawned and had my answer. If I didn't get a good night's sleep, I wouldn't have the energy to crawl across the street.

EILEEN STEPPED OUT of the elevator and spotted me in the usual crowd waiting impatiently—our building has the slowest elevators in Manhattan. She grabbed my elbow and pulled me to the center of the lobby. "Are you having trouble keeping your calendar in order?" Eileen tried to frown but the grin wouldn't stay off her face. "Or are you practicing a new skill—skipping meetings?"

As always, Eileen's mocking smile irritated me. I scowled and said, "What the hell are you talking about?"

"Our office has been invaded by people claiming they have important business to conduct with you. Only you, no one else. You have one in the reception area, driving Marcella insane, one driving Jona insane, and one in the conference room." She laughed.

"Everybody's fuming, especially the cowboy in the front."

I groaned. "Faradeux?"

"None other. Parker's hanging outside your office, fouling the air with his cigars. We put the girl in the conference room; the diamond stud in her nostril was making Faradeux nervous."

I groaned again, "Jacob Faradeux, Tony Parker, and Wina Blake?"

"Right again. At least the girl wasn't brandishing a gun." Eileen laughed and picked up her briefcase. "Have fun. It's too bad I don't have time to go up with you—I'd love to watch you handle them."

She walked out of the building, still laughing. I watched, wishing I was going with her. Just as I was wishing it would never arrive, an elevator appeared. I rode to the thirty-fourth floor, mumbling, "Faradeux. Parker. Blake. Faradeux. Parker. Blake."

My fellow passengers watched me apprehensively, trying to decide if I was dangerous. After they looked at me, they stared at their feet, not wanting to provoke the madwoman in their midst. I defiantly returned all stares. Audible sighs of relief followed me out of the elevator.

Marcella looked relieved when I stepped into the office. Faradeux bounced off the sofa and exclaimed, "Red, where have you been? If one of my hands strolled into work at ten o'clock in the morning, I'd kick his butt off my ranch."

"Good thing I'm not one of your hands. I'd kick you back."

"Now listen here—"

"Jacob, I'm a busy woman. I don't have time for your John Wayne imitations. What do you want?"

"I want to talk to you. I've been waiting for half an hour."

Faradeux's tone accused me of slacking off, wasting his money. I decided it would be a prudent move to not tell him I'd been buying birdseed for a cranky parakeet. "If you had made an appointment, I would have been here. I'll be happy to talk to you, but you'll have to wait. Other people are ahead of you."

"How long you gonna be with these more important people?"

I smiled, modeling the grin after the mocking ones Eileen flashed at me. "Half an hour, maybe a little longer. All my clients deserve my fullest attention."

"Thirty minutes, Red. I'll be back in thirty minutes. You better be ready for me 'cause I'll make John Wayne look like a sissy."

Marcella watched the exchange gleefully. We were doing our best to add excitement to her dull receptionist duties. Her eyes rolled upward with amusement; I frowned a silent reprimand. Jacob thought the frown was directed at him, and he blushed and apologized. "Okay, Red, take your time. I'll be a gentleman and wait quietly." He crushed the hat on top of his head and strode out.

One down. Two to go.

I stopped at the conference room. Wina Blake was sitting at the long table bent over a textbook with her back to the door. The music blaring through her headphones blocked out all sound. I could hear garbled lyrics warning of the coming apocalypse—cheerful music for a sixteen-year-old. I closed the door and headed to my office. Wina Blake could wait a little longer.

The putrid scent of burning dirty socks wafted around the corner. I didn't know where Tony Parker bought his cigars but he'd been ripped off: they didn't contain a shred of real tobacco. Jona looked ill. She was struggling to get away from the smoke, her glowing complexion tinted pea soup green. I had to rescue her before she barfed all over the keyboard. "Tony, I should have you arrested for assault with a deadly weapon. You didn't have to come in and foul the air. I would have been happy if you returned my phone calls."

The captain stood and attempted to blow the smoke over my head. I'm a few inches taller than he is, so the smoke streamed into my eyes. I waved the cloud away and invited Tony to enter my office.

He smiled and didn't apologize for the smoke. "You can't blame me for ducking your calls. I thought you were going to chew me out again; I wanted to give you time to cool off. I just heard you were in that fire on Avenue B. Thought I'd stop by to see if you were okay."

I opened the door to my office. "Come on in here before Jona dies from that poison you're spewing into the air." I followed Parker inside, closed the door, and leaned against it. "What do you want?"

"Now, Blaine, is that any way to act?" Tony settled on the couch and casually crossed his legs. After he finished readjusting the leg of his trousers, he looked up at me and said mildly, "I wanted to see you because I was worried about you. I wanted to be sure you weren't injured."

I shook my head and interrupted him. "Clients are stacked up all over the place waiting to see me. My office looks like LaGuardia on the night before Thanksgiving, and you're wasting my time inquiring about my health. I'm fine. Thank you for asking. Now that the polite stuff is done, tell me about the bomb in Blake's store."

Tony leaned over the coffee table and tapped the cigar against an ashtray. "There was no bomb."

"Bullshit, Tony. I went back to that store and looked around. Hurley Blake was blown to bits. I want to know what happened."

"Blaine, listen to me. There was no bomb. You were lucky to get out of that inferno without getting hurt."

What I saw in his face startled me. I blurted out, "You're afraid."

Tony stood, pushed his voice to a lower level and in a rush of words, said, "I'm doing you a favor and I don't know why. I'm always doing favors for you but you never listen. You have an overactive imagination that's going to get you killed someday. Believe me, it was a fire."

"Who investigated?"

"No way. Forget it. I'm not going to allow you to pester my staff with stupid questions. Why don't you take care of your rich clients? Leave the garbage cases to us dedicated civil servants." He pushed past me and was gone before I could answer.

I wanted to sit and think but I knew Faradeux wouldn't be able to wait much longer. My cowboy was probably back in the lobby, impatiently torturing his hat as he waited. I buzzed Jona, asked her to fetch him, and pretended to study the papers on my desk.

Ten-gallon hat in hand, Faradeux strode into my office. He waved a calloused hand at me and boomed, "Don't get up, Red. A pretty little lady like you shouldn't stand for an ugly old coot like me."

Faradeux tossed the black hat on my desk and sat down. "I called Nanci. She told me to start by apologizing for acting like a boor. Frankly, I'm a little embarrassed 'bout this situation. I always handle my problems myself, I'm not used to relying on strangers. Especially women."

I murmured a gracious reply, then said, "I thought you'd be back in Texas by now."

"I'm staying another day or two. My investment bankers want to impress me by flashing big numbers on their overhead projectors. I never thought I'd wake up of a morning and find big-city investment bankers drooling over my herds. But to tell you the God's honest truth, Red, I'm worried. Everybody at Faradeux Industries works hard and works honest. I don't want to see their efforts vilified by a group of leaf-eaters."

"I went to a leaf-eaters meeting last night. They showed a very graphic film of your operation. It wasn't very sympathetic to your cause."

Faradeux mournfully shook his head and drawled, "State of the art, Red. We follow every damn code invented by every damn agency in this country."

A discussion of his business would only waste time. I asked, "What do you want?" and tried to remember how many times I'd used that phrase. Maybe Ida would lend me Mikey for a few days: he could sit on my desk and repeat "What do you want?" to everyone who came near him. I could go sit on a beach in the Caribbean, work on my tan, and ask questions like "When do they start serving lunch?" or "Would you rub suntan lotion on my back?"

Faradeux was talking; I brought myself back from the islands. "We received another letter from that group; it was sent by one of those overnight services. Nanci faxed it to me. I thought you should see it."

The letter warned against the involvement of "highly paid professional lackeys. They will not sway us from condemning your speciesism." The communiqué ended with WARM's standard disclaimer protesting the use of innocent animals for man's profit.

"It's been a long time since I've been called a professional lackey. Jacob, you have a leak down in Texas. Who knows you hired my firm?"

"I cannot believe that one of my people would be disloyal to me." Jacob folded his arms across his chest, ending the discussion.

"Sorry, Jacob. That's not good enough. Someone from your company is sharing information with WARM. It took them less than twenty-four hours to learn that you hired us. Who, besides Nanci, knows we're involved?"

"You worry about Manhattan. I'll worry about Texas."

I wanted to throw him out, but I had signed a contract, made a commitment, and deposited the check. "You hired me for my expertise, so listen to me. Keep all communication between us confidential. Don't trust anyone. I went to a WARM meeting last night; they don't like you or your company. Let's not make things easier for them by leaking our plans." Faradeux sputtered; I cut him off. "Think about who's talking. Plugging your leak could save us a lot of grief.''

Jacob shook his head. "I cannot believe that one of my people would be disloyal to me.''

"So you say. When are you going back to Texas?'' I wanted Faradeux out of Manhattan before he exploded and went charging into WARM's offices to set them straight.

"I'm leaving this afternoon but I'll be back next week. I'll want to know what progress you've made.''

"Just make an appointment, I'll be here.'' I smiled and held out my hand. Faradeux grinned, seized my hand with an iron grip, and pumped it.

"See you next week, Red.''

Jona escorted Faradeux out. I watched and rubbed my temples—my chronic headache, fueled by too many cigarettes, returned. The pain reminded me of Wina Blake. It was time to see how she was amusing herself.

Wina was still working, bent over a textbook with her back to the door. Rhythmic bass and drums buzzed from beneath the foam-padded headphones covering her ears. I walked over and tapped her on the shoulder.

Wina pulled the headphones off and wrapped them around her neck. Rap music blasted out from the black foam pads. She snapped the player off and glared at me.

"Sorry, I didn't mean to startle you.'' I slid into a chair next to her and looked at the book on the table. Chemistry—a subject I had hated and always flirted with failing. "Are you hungry? I just ordered a pizza. I was wondering if you'd like to share it with me.''

Wina stiffened. "Don't have no money."

"I didn't ask for money. I asked if you would like some pizza—I can't eat a whole pie by myself." The girl mumbled something that could have been either a curse or agreement. I smiled like an idiot and went on. "Are you still studying or are you ready to take a break?"

"Study."

"Okay. My office is next door. I'll let you know when the pizza gets here."

Wina waited five minutes so I'd understand that she wasn't jumping at my command, then strolled into my office. She threw herself into a chair and snatched a crystal paper-weight, an anniversary present from my husband, from my desk. I removed it from her hands and carefully held it out of reach.

She didn't say anything. Neither did I. Wina stared out the window; I stared at her.

"What you looking at?"

"I didn't expect to see you again. Last time we met, you tossed my card into a puddle and ran away."

Wina's eyes darted across my face; she almost smiled. "Went back and picked it up."

"Why aren't you in school?"

"Finals. Got a chemistry exam in two days. Gotta study hard for it. Study hall too noisy. You gonna throw me out?"

"No, I won't throw you out. You can study here. You can use the conference room whenever it's empty. My secretary can find you an empty office if the room is booked. Just don't ask me for help."

"What?" Her eyes widened.

"I hate chemistry. Don't ask me to help with your homework."

Wina wanted to ask for more than a place to study, but we were interrupted before I could press her. The pizza man dumped his cardboard box on the table and started to tell me his latest joke. I don't know the pizza man's name but I love his jokes. Not today. I cut him off and hustled him out, but the moment was lost—Wina didn't feel like talking anymore.

I spread the plates out and distributed pizza while Wina poured soda. Chores completed, we sat back and started to eat. I took a small bite. Vivid memories of WARM's movie came to mind; I couldn't swallow. I picked the sausage off and took another, smaller bite and nearly choked. All my desire for lunch had disappeared. I put the pizza down and watched my guest.

Wina tore through one slice and eagerly grabbed another. After she finished, I put a third piece on her plate and asked, "What do you want? It's a long trip up here for nothing more than a place to study."

"Nothing. I don't want nothing." She devoured the pizza in a few bites and glanced at the open box. I dumped a fourth piece on her plate and said, "You came all the way up here to study? Isn't this a little out of your way?"

"I want you to help me. Find out who killed my daddy."

"Wina—"

She threw the half-eaten slice of pizza down. It bounced off the plate and skidded across the table, leaving a trail of grease behind. "Nobody cares 'bout a dead black man—one less nigger to keep down."

"That's enough." I slapped an open palm against the table. "I don't want to hear—"

"But the system—"

"The system didn't kill your father. Maybe it's not investigating fast enough for you, but—"

"No investigation. The fire started in the wiring; it was an accident."

"Who told you that?"

"The police. I called them this morning." In a singsong rapper's voice, she chanted, "There will be no investigation. We won't repeat this conversation. The sparks came from the wire overhead." She started to cry. "They told me to stop calling. They said I was wasting their time...."

FOUR

THE SUBWAY JERKED to a standstill in the middle of a tunnel. It's something you can count on happening whenever you're in a hurry. The Transit Authority has a sixth sense about these things—they yank the plug and let you sit for a while to think about your hectic lifestyle. It's part of their efforts to reduce stressful living in the Big Apple. I thought about being late and my wasted fare. None of my thoughts were charitable.

The lights flickered; the air conditioner whined and returned to full strength. It was a tease; after thirty seconds everything died. Simultaneous curses, groans, and nervous laughter filled the car and quickly faded to silence. We were too accustomed to being stranded beneath the sidewalks of Manhattan to complain for long. Better to save your strength for the next hassle.

The conductor's announcement was garbled beyond comprehension. The subdued muttering swelled to catcalls and once again slowly died to silence. We stood, or sat if lucky, in the darkness, quietly sweating, fuming, and vowing never again to ride a subway. It was a promise most of us would soon forget—until the next time we got stuck in a tunnel.

After ten or fifteen endless minutes, the train lurched into action. We inched to Twenty-third Street without another delay. I pushed through the impatient crowd on the platform and ran up to the street, looking at my watch as I sprinted to the WARM office.

The elevator was working this time, and I rode alone up to the sixth floor. The outer door to the WARM office was ajar. Roz and Grant were sitting at the battered conference table; neither one noticed me slip inside.

"You're such an idiot. What the hell were you thinking?"

"I was thinking of the group. She has money. She'll be an asset."

"Bullshit!"

Grant smiled and said, "What's the matter? Are you jealous?"

I would have slapped the smile from his face but Roz didn't flinch. "No, I'm not jealous. You've had your flings before but you never let it hurt the group—until now. Inviting her to this meeting was stupid. You've been blinded by a cute piece of ass. That scares me."

Activism as a way of picking up chicks? I smiled and thought, Thanks for the compliment, but didn't take offense—eavesdroppers can't argue with what they overhear. I backed out, tapped on the door, and cheerfully called, "Hello! Is there anybody here? Am I too early?"

Grant put a warning hand on Roz's forearm. "Blaine, come in. You're right on time, everyone else is late." He patted the chair at his side. "Sit down. The others will be here soon."

I sat. Grant jumped up and fussed around the coffeepot, pretending to make coffee. Roz grimaced at me. It was meant to be a friendly greeting, so I smiled.

"It's very unusual for someone to join the committee after only one meeting. Grant was very impressed with you."

She was thinking, He was impressed with your ass. I fixed an artificial smile on my face and waited.

"Tell me about yourself." Roz crossed her arms across her chest, daring me to impress her.

I shrugged. "There isn't much to tell. I've finally gotten disgusted enough to take a stand. We can't belittle the pain and suffering nonhumans are subjected to because of our insatiable desire for hamburgers. I'm sick of being passive." Realizing that I was dangerously close to sounding like an insincere idiot, I paused and tired to think of a coherent way out.

The noise of other people entering the room saved me. We turned to the doorway. Grant stood with three people, two men and a woman. Roz flushed but introduced them without snarling.

The woman, Amy, had been snatched from the sixties and dropped in present-day Manhattan still wearing her denim skirt, tie-dyed blouse, and wire-rimmed glasses. Long, freshly permed curls exploded around her head. They bobbed as she nodded her welcome.

The men, Collier Whitehead and Harold Hodgkins, were nearly identical twins who had also been transported from a different place and time. Not from the sixties, but from an L.L. Bean catalog. Tall, sporting healthy tans, handsome, it was hard to distinguish between the two, except where Hodgkins had dark curly hair, most of Whitehead's hair was gone. Collier was tall, Harold was taller. They were dressed in matching pleated slacks and striped cotton shirts, clothes more appropriate for an afternoon of sailing than an evening of planning to disrupt the food chain.

The taller, thinner one—Harold—tossed his brief-case on the table and sat next to me. He abruptly turned to examine my face. "Haven't we met? You look familiar."

I laughed. "Everyone in Manhattan looks familiar. We probably fought over a taxi the other night." I paused for a second, then said, "You won the cab, left me standing in the rain."

It's too bad you don't win awards for undercover performances; I would have walked away with a little gold statue. Everyone laughed, and Hodgkins grunted and turned away.

Roz waited for the laughter to end before she persisted, "You haven't finished telling me about yourself."

"Roz," Grant interrupted, "we have a lot of work to do tonight."

"She's new. It's important to trust her."

Amy's uncertain voice intruded before Grant could reply. "I agree with Roz. We should know Blaine better before we talk about business. Of course, I trust Grant's judgment too."

One of the men asked me a question, breaking open the floodgates. Question after question came at me until my head was spinning from the strain of keeping my lies untangled. I spit out key phrases from the brochures and added a few ringing passages of my own, hoping to convince them of my sincerity.

Grant didn't participate; he didn't even pay attention. He lounged in a chair at the head of the table, reading a Greenpeace newsletter. When the pace of questioning slowed, he dropped the newsletter on the floor and pointedly looked at his watch. "We are wasting time. Are you all happy now?"

Precise Mr. Whitehead, who should have been called Mr. Baldhead, held up a hand. "Just a minute, Grant." He looked at me and said, "You didn't sign the registration sheet last night."

"Was there one? I guess I missed it." I shrugged and smiled. "Sorry."

"Well?" Roz impatiently clattered her fingernails against the table. When I didn't answer, she snapped, "Where do you live? What's your phone number? Where do you work?"

"I live in the Village." And I recited the number of an answering service I keep for these special occasions. My buddies at the service take special precautions to be sure the number can't be traced to me.

Roz ignored the sweet smile I flashed at her. "What about a work number?"

"I don't work."

"What do you mean you don't work? Are you independently wealthy?"

"My husband died a few years ago. We weren't rich but he believed in life insurance. It's not a lot of money. Jeff always said he didn't want me to be forced to go back to work if something happened to him."

A few tears would have been a nice touch, but I don't have the ability to cry on demand. Instead of crying, I looked down at my hands. They were shaking.

The money I have is mine, earned through hard work and good investments. The only money Jeff left was a very small insurance policy and worthless penny stocks. But no one needed to know that. I made believe I was trying to hide my shaking hands and looked around the table.

They believed my lies. Isn't it amazing how a healthy bank account can win the respect of the people who want to tap into it? An "I told you so" look arced between Grant and Roz. A rich widow, ready for Grant's special attention, would be graciously welcomed by all, even Roz. Everyone smiled and relaxed.

Baldhead started a boring report, sounding more like a board member from a Fortune 500 company than a revolutionary fighting to change an oppressive suzerain. "Renkel's Furs on Fifth Avenue is showing its winter line next week. We can't stop them. We can get a lot of publicity."

Whitehead's report went on forever. Assignments, traffic patterns, media coverage. My eyelids drooped. The others, except Grant, were vitally interested in every word. Grant idly colored the scratches on the table top with his pencil, occasionally smirking. When Whitehead finally paused to catch his breath, Grant dropped the pencil. Into the silence, he said, "Let's blow the fuckers up."

"THE MEETING ENDED in bedlam."

"Uh huh..."

"Eileen, I called for advice, not absentminded grunts." I waited for an answer and received an earful of static. "Something's bothering you. What's wrong? You sound worried."

"Nothing's wrong." She sighed. "It's been a long day. I'm tired."

"It's after nine. Go home. We'll talk in the morning."

We hung up. I sorted the mail into piles of junk and bills—that's all I ever receive. People don't write letters anymore. Who can afford the postage? I quickly gave up and tossed the envelopes on the kitchen table. Eileen's lack of attention still annoyed me. I paced around the kitchen, thinking. I decided to go to the View; maybe Bobby or Ryan would be interested in my troubles.

It's handy having a bar on the corner—cuts down on the commuting time. I walked in and smiled. A thick haze of cigarette and pipe smoke hung inches from the ceiling—no nonsmoking section at the View. Check your lungs outside; no one cares if you're allergic to the blue fumes. Bobby and Ryan are allergic to people who complain about secondhand smoke.

Ryan's hand hovered over the tap, a mug poised beneath the spigot. I shook my head. A beer would be heaven, but I wasn't ready to take a tumble off the wagon. Ryan slid a mug of seltzer to me. I sank onto a stool and lit a cigarette.

"Blaine." The well-being I was trying to build up evaporated. I turned and looked into Dennis Halstead's brown eyes. "You're hard to find."

I felt a flash of guilt for not returning his calls and tried to cover it by smiling. "Sorry. Jona told me you called, but my office has been a madhouse. I didn't forget you, I was planning to call you in the morning."

"I know you, you tossed my messages on your desk and forgot about them. There used to be a time when you'd call me back seconds after I hung up."

"That was a long time ago, Dennis. Things have changed."

"You haven't."

He gently touched my back and let his hand slip down to my hips. I stiffened and moved away.

"Thanks for not noticing the wrinkles. But take a good look; I'm not the same person you used to sleep with. I've been married. Widowed. I lost a baby. I drank enough booze to empty a distillery." Dennis frowned, but I wasn't ready to stop. "Is that enough? Do you still want to talk about the good old days?"

"You are a stubborn idiot with a tendency to self-pity."

His smile took the sting from his words. "It's your most endearing quality. I'm never bored when I'm with you."

"Charm boy."

He shrugged. "It's my most endearing quality. Tall redheads are especially susceptible to my charm. You're the tallest redhead in here, what do you think?"

Dennis smiled again. I frowned and said, "Take your charm and turn it on some underage bimbo who'll be impressed. I like you better when you're not trying to be enchanting."

His face flushed with anger. I swiveled around and swallowed a mouthful of seltzer. Dennis didn't go away. I put the mug down on the bar and turned back to him. "This isn't your usual type of hangout. Why are you slumming?"

"Your secretary told me you'd gone home. When you didn't answer the door, I decided to look here." Dennis glanced over my shoulder at the glass on the bar. I noticed but didn't comment. The View had been a favorite hideout in my drinking days; Dennis was only checking.

I smiled and said, "Thanks for sending Faradeux to me—he's a real character."

"Faradeux?" Dennis laughed. "That ole cowboy? I'm afraid he's a paranoid fool. He kept pestering me for the name of somebody who could help him. I thought I was doing you a favor. Guess I should have warned you."

"Thanks anyway." I caught Ryan's eye, pointed at Dennis, and mimicked filling a beer mug. "Let me buy you a drink. We always appreciate another paying customer, even if he is a little weird. Do you think there's anything to Faradeux's worries about his ceremony at the Exchange?"

"No—"

Ryan interrupted Dennis's answer. "Here's your beer and here's another seltzer for the lady. Who's paying?"

The View doesn't believe in running tabs during the evening hours; their pay-as-you-drink-it policy goes into effect at six o'clock. I silently handed Ryan a few bills from the little pile I had on the bar and passed the beer to Dennis.

He took the mug and looked around the room. "It's too noisy up here, let's get a booth before they're all taken. I have to talk to you."

After leaving a good tip for Ryan, I stuck my change in my pocket, grabbed my cigarettes and drink, and reluctantly followed Dennis to the back of the bar. He waited politely for me to sit and took the seat opposite me.

Dennis wiped condensation from the mug with his index finger. Without looking up he asked, "What are you working on these days?"

"J. Edgar's dead and buried—I don't have to answer that."

Dennis frowned. He pushed the mug aside and said, "I hate this stuff." I wasn't sure if he was talking about the beer or my answer. "Let's stop playing games. A lot of people know we used to..."

Dennis fumbled for the correct phrase. I waited, curious to hear his description of what we used to be. "We used to be close. I don't know what you're working on, but I think you should concentrate on Faradeux. Forget everything else."

"What are you talking about? Faradeux and his desire to have a happy celebration is the only case I'm working on. I haven't talked to you for months. Why are you suddenly so interested in my career?" The whirlwind in my head picked up speed. "You're talking about Hurley Blake, aren't you? What do you care about a burnt-out bodega on Avenue B?"

Dennis looked puzzled. He asked, "Who's Hurley Blake?"

I stared at him incredulously. "If it's not Blake, then what are you talking about?"

"I don't know. I heard you've been pissing people off again—which doesn't surprise me. I thought I'd talk to you before you got into real trouble." He shrugged. "I don't have any sinister intentions. This is simply another misguided attempt to do you a favor."

Too many people were trying to do me favors. Telling myself I should be thankful for his outburst of goodwill, I decided to be nice. I was never good at apologizing to Dennis, but I did try. "I appreciate your concern, but I haven't done anything to get the FBI mad at me. You shouldn't pay attention to the gossip around the watercooler. Thanks anyway." I tossed some money on the table and said, "I'm going home. I need to catch up on my sleep."

Dennis didn't offer to accompany me. I wandered home, alone and confused, wondering why Dennis was trying to be helpful and why I cared. Suddenly exhausted, I dragged myself up the stairs to my bedroom, turned off the bedside phone, and crawled into bed.

NOISE FROM THE STREET below my bedroom window woke me. It was nearly three o'clock and the last drunken, rowdy customers from the View were tumbling out onto the street.

Tumbling wasn't a figure of speech. Four people, three men and a woman, were performing somersaults in the middle of Barrow Street. Each roll was accompanied by shouting, cheering, and a loud "Umphff" as the gymnast landed on the hard pavement. Somersaults were quickly replaced by a less painful game of leapfrog.

Despite Bobby and Ryan's attempts to keep peace with the neighbors, the View had a few boisterous patrons who drank rivers of beer and didn't care if their noise fueled an increasingly antagonistic relationship with the quiet Village neighborhood. I sat on the wide windowsill and watched, wondering how long it would take for the local precinct to respond to the irate calls that were undoubtedly lighting up the switchboard.

The cops were quick. Ida, who usually calls them, must have installed speed dialing. I could picture her peering out from behind her heavy bedroom curtains, smiling with delight as a police car floated around the corner. Flashing streaks of red, yellow, and white from the rooftop lights illuminated the gamesome quartet. They hopped to the curb and leaned against a parked car, giggling and waiting for a stern lecture. The police car stopped in front of my house. The officer who got out ignored them and climbed my stairs.

I jumped down from the windowsill and headed for the closet. The buzzer sounded as I was pulling on a terry cloth robe. I ran down the stairs, already worrying. The police don't visit in the middle of the night to announce that you've won the lottery.

There was a second, quick stab at the buzzer, followed by a thirty-second thrust at the bell. Thirty seconds is a long time for an annoying buzzer to sound, especially at three o'clock in the morning.

"Dammit, give me a break." I fumbled with the robe's belt with one hand and attempted to turn the locks with the other. I finally managed to slide the last bolt free and pulled the door open.

"Blaine, you shouldn't open the door so quickly. It could be a bad guy."

"Jose." I recognized the patrolman from my days on the force. We shared a patrol car for a week when his regular partner was on sick leave. "The bad guys don't usually drive up in a police car with the lights flashing. What's the matter? Are you and your partner bored?"

He didn't laugh. The knot in my stomach, the knot I was trying to ignore, twisted. "Can I come in?" I wordlessly stepped back and let him inside. "Captain Parker sent us. He's been trying to call you."

"I turned off the phone and crawled into bed around ten." My hands trembled. I stuffed them into my pockets and said, "What's wrong?"

"There's been an...accident." I clenched my hands into tight, nervous fists and sagged against the wall. I didn't have the strength to hear this again.

"No, it wasn't an accident." Jose slipped into an official police tone. "At approximately ten forty-five this evening, a bomb exploded in your office."

"A bomb!" I bounced off the wall. "Was anyone hurt?"

Jose's dark eyes reflected my worried face. "The bomb exploded in your sister's office. She was there when it went off."

"How serious..." I couldn't finish. Too many horrible images rushed through my head.

"I don't know. She's at St. Katherine's Trauma Center. The captain said we should take you there."

I moved to the door. Jose grabbed my arm and gestured at my naked legs and bare feet. "Put some clothes on. I'll wait down here."

FIVE

THE RIDE UPTOWN was a nightmare. We rocketed through the rutted streets in the police capsule, its revolving lights excusing us from stopping at red traffic signals. There wasn't any need for the siren; the few cars on the road scurried out of our way without any prompting.

I closed my eyes and rested my head against the seat cushion, straining to keep from thinking. We pulled up to the emergency room entrance. I jumped out and was inside before the car stopped moving. The seats were filled with other people who had given up and were waiting for someone to call their names for treatment. A few hardy people wandered around looking for a sympathetic face; I joined the search. A resident hurried past, and I grabbed her arm and began to ask a question. She brushed my hand away and snapped, "Tell it to a nurse."

Good advice. I found a nurse, who flipped through a chart and said, "She's not here anymore; she's in surgery. Go up to the third floor family lounge; you can wait there. Her husband went up a little while ago."

"Can you tell me—"

"I can't tell you anything. Elevators are down there." She pointed down the hall and turned away. More important matters demanded her attention.

Too frantic to wait for an elevator, I sprinted up the stairs. The lounge was at the far end of the deserted corridor. I flew down it and into the waiting room.

"Blaine—"

I ran across the floor into the arms of Eileen's husband. We clung to each other without speaking. Don's arms trembled. I could feel—no, I could smell the fear rising from deep within his body.

"Don, how's Eileen? What happened?"

"I...I don't know. She's in surgery. They haven't been able to tell me much." Don's voice cracked. "It's bad."

The three women stationed in the corner of the room put down the box of tissues they were passing among them and watched us with interest. I glowered at them; they didn't flinch. Seeking privacy, I grabbed Don's arm and dragged him out to the corridor, away from their prying eyes. I pointed at the vending machines at the end of the hallway and suggested coffee. Don agreed and slowly followed me.

I slid quarters into the machine and watched liquid splash into the cardboard cup. Don took the cup while I fed four more coins to the machine for a second cup. As soon as I picked up the container, I knew I'd made a mistake. The brackish liquid couldn't be coffee. It looked and smelled like water from the East River. Now, I've never actually tasted water from the East River, but I was positive the muck from the machine would taste worse.

I dumped the cup in the trash and turned to Don. "What happened?"

"Eileen called me around ten-thirty. We were arguing because she was working so late...she's been working too much lately. No one else was there, everyone else went home at a normal hour. The bell rang." Our office doors are locked at five—anyone who wants to get in after that has to ring a bell. "Eileen put the phone down—"

Coffee splashed from Don's cup and landed on the floor between us. Don looked at his shaking hands, surprised to find them trying to hold the cup. He dropped it in the garbage. "She came back after a few minutes and said somebody had left a package. She tossed it on the desk. I heard the explosion...."

Don mumbled something. I was going to ask another question but he turned and trudged down the empty corridor to the lounge, anxious to resume his watch. I followed, a million questions he couldn't answer ringing inside my head.

The scene in the waiting room hadn't changed. A few more people had joined the others. They were sitting in the corners, quietly talking and crying. The three women hadn't moved from their perches, Elvis Presley was still dancing through the static on the television screen, and the air was still filled with smoke from nervous chain-smokers.

We sat and quickly became enveloped in the rigid protocol of the family lounge limbo. If you need to talk, the others gratefully put aside their fears and listen to yours. If you need to cry, they silently pass tissues. If you want to bend over and stare at your feet, they form a respectful circle of empty chairs around you and glare at anyone who dares to breach the linoleum moat.

People drifted in and out; no one came near us. Don hunched over in his seat and stared at his running shoes, fascinated by the fraying laces. I fidgeted on the unyielding plastic, chain-smoking and worrying. An hour dragged by without any word.

I smoked another cigarette, dropped the butt into the overflowing stand, and looked at my watch. It was impossible to sit any longer. I jumped to my feet. "It's been over an hour. I'm going to find out what's happening." I stalked out and began a vicious game of hide-and-seek.

It was a frustrating and fruitless search. The corridors were empty, the people with the answers in hiding. The nurse guarding the doorway to the intensive care unit smiled and shrugged when I demanded answers.

I walked past a lonely porter diligently mopping the floor, slammed into the lounge, and threw myself in the chair next to Don. Seconds later I was back on my feet, pacing across the floor. Fourteen steps from the windows to the door, fourteen steps back.

Windows to the door. Door to the windows. Windows to the door. Door to the windows.

I was looking down at a very empty First Avenue when the soft chatter abruptly ended, signaling an intruder. Dr. Mabe, her dark hair glittering with sweat, motioned for us to join her in the hall. We rushed across the room, eager and afraid.

"Eileen's out of surgery. They'll be bringing her up soon. You'll be able to see her—for a few minutes."

Don and I spoke at the same time. "How is she?"

"Stable, but guarded."

"What the hell does that mean?"

Dr. Mabe glared at me. "She's alive. Eileen was very close to the bomb when it exploded. She has a number of deep puncture wounds and internal bleeding. Shrapnel lodged in her eyes."

"How bad?"

"Don, we just don't know."

Time and other wait-and-see words floated around my head. I'm not good at waiting. I ran out of the hospital.

The bright sunlight startled me. I expected to find darkness, everything frozen in place, suspended until our drama reached an end. Crowds of people hurrying to their jobs swirled around me, reminding me that it was the start of a new day. I stood on the sidewalk, blinking in the sunlight and hearing Grant's voice: "Let's blow the fuckers up." An icy rage, the worst kind, engulfed me. If WARM was involved, I'd find out.

THE OFFICE WAS strangely quiet. The technicians and police had finished their chores and disappeared, leaving nothing but a tape stretched across the entrance to Eileen's office. I was about to duck under the ribbon when a voice from down the hallway stopped me.

"Hey, Babe." The voice belonged to Brad Carlson, and the sight of his ex-linebacker's frame rushing toward me was reassuring. No one else on my staff would attempt to call me Babe, but Brad does; he enjoys watching me grit my teeth at the sound of his nickname. We've known each other for over thirty years—we met in nursery school. On the first day of our acquaintance, Brad tried to break an easel over my head because I stole his paintbrush. I knocked him on his butt and was stomping on his chest when the teacher intervened. Brad and I sniveled at each other from opposite ends of the playground and have remained friends ever since. When a training camp injury ended Brad's pro-football career, he joined my staff.

Brad wrapped his massive arms around my shoulders and crushed me against his chest. "How's Eileen?"

I closed my eyes and mumbled into his shirt. "She...I don't know.... Brad—I don't trust the security guards at the hospital. They're well-meaning but they're amateurs. Would you keep an eye on her? I know you don't like to do bodyguard work, but..."

"Hey, Babe, don't sweat it. I'd be pissed if you asked somebody else. I only hope I get a chance to whack the bastard."

"Don't whack anybody. Just take care of Eileen."

"Okay, Babe, message received. I'll call for your permission before I whack anyone. What are you going to do?"

"I don't know." I yawned and realized how drained I felt; it was difficult to complete a thought. "Poke around. Follow up on a few things."

Brad pushed me away and stared at me. "Do you have a lead? Share it with me."

"No, I don't have a lead." I wasn't ready to share my feelings about WARM with anyone, especially Brad. If I mentioned my suspicions, he'd be all over Wilder and friends before I could stop him. I held back for a selfish reason: I wanted to be the first one there. "Nothing concrete."

"Yeah, sure, Babe. You're the boss, I have to believe you. Just be sure to call me before the fun starts."

"Brad—"

"Take it easy, I was joking. Where's your sense of humor?"

"Somebody blew it up last night."

He thumped my back. It was meant to be a reassuring gesture. "You be careful."

"Yessir, I'll be careful. Thanks for your concern. Take good care of Eileen." I started for her office.

Brad grabbed my arm. "Wait a second. Have you been in there yet?"

I was too tired to argue, too tired to answer. I shook my head.

"Don't. It's a real mess. That guy meant business."

"Brad, tell me something I don't know. Remember, I spent the night at the hospital, waiting for the results. I think I can handle seeing the mess."

"Listen to me, Babe. You've been up all night. You're upset and tired. I don't think you're in any shape to pick through the rubble. Leave it alone for a while."

Brad was doing his best, but I refused to listen. I childishly folded my arms and repeated, "No."

"Okay, be stubborn. I'll go with you."

"Don't waste your time. Go the hospital and watch out for Eileen. I can take care of myself."

"Sure you can take care of yourself. Where's your gun?"

My head hurt when I tried to think. I rubbed my forehead to clear the fog, and said, "What are you talking about?"

If an easel had been within reach, Brad would have cracked it over my head. He sighed and patiently explained, "Babe, somebody just tried to kill your sister. He might have your name on his list. Have you thought about that?"

"I haven't thought—"

"That's what I figured. Where's your gun?"

"Home." My brand-new Smith & Wesson 9-mm automatic was home, securely locked in its case. It had only been out for practice at the pistol range and I wasn't anxious to take it out for anything else. I don't like guns.

Brad wisely let that argument fade. He pounded my back once again and said, "Well, think about it, Babe. You need to take care of yourself. I'll be at the hospital, call if you need reinforcements."

I ducked under the ribbon stretched across the opening and flicked on the overhead lights. After a dozen years of working as first a cop, then a private investigator, I've seen too many blood-spattered rooms to be upset by them. Each time I view the aftermath of a violent attack, my stomach, hardened by repeated exposure to the gore, turns a little less violently.

It's different when the bloodstains were left by your sister. The sight of the splintered desk and bloody carpet sickened me. My head spun; a black veil threatened to drop over my eyes. I was going to faint. This was worse, much worse than I had imagined. I fought to catch my breath and wished Brad had been more forceful in trying to keep me out of the room. I wished I had listened to him.

I righted Eileen's chair and sat down, idly poking at the debris with my toes while I caught my breath and surveyed the room. It was a mess. The desk was smashed; books, papers, and mementos were scattered across the floor. Even though I knew the cops had sifted through rubble carefully during the night, I slid to my knees and examined the wreckage. I needed to touch it, to feel it—to find something that would unwaveringly point me to WARM.

My fingers nudged a picture frame, and I pulled it free. The webbed cracks in the glass made it difficult to interpret the scene, but I recognized the picture. I had been the photographer on that sunny beach weekend when everyone's life was happier. Eileen, Don, and Jeff playing in the surf.

"Blaine." Jona was leaning over the police tape, anxiously trying to get my attention. "Dennis Halstead is here to see you."

"Send him to my office. I'll meet you there." I tucked the photo under my arm and crunched through the glass and wood, thinking I would get a new frame and take it to the hospital to cheer Eileen up. The thought that she might not be able to see it was too sour to dwell on; I forced my mind away from the hospital.

I tossed the picture onto my desk, where it landed face down. I frowned and didn't bother to turn it over. My frown deepened when Dennis Halstead stood to greet me. As usual, Dennis looked more like a *GQ* model than an FBI agent. His double-breasted suit, silk tie, and crisp white shirt made me uncomfortably aware of my faded blue jeans and rumpled polo shirt. He smiled as if he could read my mind, and I blushed and closed the door.

"Would you like a cup of coffee?" I'll admit it wasn't a memorable opening line, but I was tired and nervous. Having Dennis turn up two days in a row added to my jitters.

"Sure—black."

I remembered.

I poured two cups from the always-full pot on the credenza and sank into the chair behind my desk. Dennis took a sip of coffee to be polite, then put the cup down, carefully using an empty ashtray as a coaster.

"What was Eileen working on?"

I groaned. "Didn't we have a similar conversation yesterday? Don't you ever give up?"

"Come on, Blaine, give me a break. We're on the same side on this one."

"Are we? It's hard to tell. Who sent you this time? I wish you'd tell your bosses we aren't an item any-more—maybe they'll stop ordering you to follow me around."

Dennis didn't lose his temper. He should have, but he didn't. Instead of yelling, Dennis said calmly, "No one sent me. It's my case. Holding back information won't help Eileen."

"Same old Dennis, still looking for help so you don't have to get your hands dirty. Do something constructive, go browbeat somebody who will be impressed by your badge."

"And you're still a coldhearted bitch." He walked to the doorway and paused for one last try. "Call me if you change your mind—you know the number."

"Presumptuous, don't you think? I don't know your number. Leave a card with my secretary in case I decide to call."

He slammed the door behind him. Dennis always slammed the door after losing an argument. I smiled, happy with my small victory. Jona's grave voice interrupted my short celebration. "Brad's on the phone."

Panic hit. Brad was calling to tell me Eileen was dead. My hand wouldn't move—it refused to pick up the telephone. Jona's worried voice came through the intercom again. "Do you want to take the call?"

No, I didn't want to take the call. Why should I take the call? He was going to tell me Eileen was dead. I grabbed the receiver. My hands were trembling, but somehow I managed to keep my voice from quavering. "Brad, what's wrong?"

"Babe, you'd better get over here." I braced myself for the bad news. "There's some bleeding. It won't stop. They're talking about taking her back into surgery. She's been asking for you. You should come before they operate."

THE ROOM WAS DARK. Heavy green drapes blocked the sunlight and muted the sounds of construction from the street below. I wanted to look out the window or pace around the sterile room. I wanted to do anything that would give me reason to turn away from the bed.

Instead of giving in to the urge to flee, I moved closer to the bed and gently cradled Eileen's unresponsive hand in mine. She floated in and out of awareness, and only once was lucid enough to realize I was at her side. That one lucid moment changed everything. All my plans to go after WARM disappeared when Eileen squeezed my hand and whispered, "Rudy. MacIntyre."

I didn't know the name but that didn't matter. I stroked Eileen's hand and whispered, "I'll find him."

Her hand went limp. I repeated, "I'll find him," and sat back to watch and wait. I didn't cry until after the nurses gently asked me to leave. Brad and Don were standing outside the ICU. They both reached out to me, but I swatted their outstretched hands away and blindly stumbled into the lounge. They barricaded the doors and left me alone.

I sat in the empty room and cried.

SIX

FOOTSTEPS HESITATED in the doorway; Parker walked in, somehow having managed to talk his way past the men blocking the door. He knelt in front of the chair and tried to embrace me. I ducked, stood up, and turned away from him to look out the window.

"How is Eileen?" I shook my head and continued to stare out the window. Parker joined me. "Do you have any ideas?"

"No."

"Nothing?"

I shook my head again and whispered, "Nothing."

Parker unwrapped a cigar and stuck it in his mouth. "That's hard for me to believe. I would have bet you'd be after a dozen people by now, accusing them of sending that bomb to your sister."

"That would be a sucker bet. Tony, can this wait? I don't feel like talking."

Parker joined the ranks of people who can't take a hint. He touched my arm and said, "Come on, I'm trying to find a killer."

"Dammit, she's not dead yet!" I shook his hand from my arm and shouted, "What the hell do you care? You were the last person I heard threatening Eileen. Maybe I should investigate you."

"Now listen here—"

"Something wrong, folks?" Brad's head popped into the room. "There's a lot of noise echoing around

the hallway, the nurses are starting to get annoyed."
He walked over to us and peered into my eyes. "Are
you okay?"

"She's not okay. She's nuts." Parker was panting,
waving his cigar in the air.

"Nuts! You want to see nuts?" I snatched the cigar
from his hand, tore it apart, and threw the pieces at his
chest. "That's nuts."

"You stupid— Just watch how fast this investigation goes down the toilet." Parker sputtered to silence, encouraged by the heavy hand Brad dropped on
his shoulder. He flicked a shred of tobacco from his tie
and stomped from the room.

Brad watched him leave, then turned to me. "Nice
going, Babe. You ruined the man's cigar. Spoiled his
good mood too. Great way to alienate the cops. Do
you feel better?" I nodded. I did feel better. Brad
grinned. "Good, there's nothing like a temper tantrum to take your mind off your troubles. Make
somebody else miserable, that's my motto. Come on,
sit down and get hold of yourself. I sent Don for coffee, he should be back soon. He doesn't need to see
you upset like this."

Brad guided me back to the orange seats, where we
sat in the quiet room without talking. The quiet lasted
a few minutes, and ended when I realized we were sitting a death watch. I pulled my hand away, jumped
up, and ran out before Brad could stop me. If Eileen
was going to die, she would die—sitting in the waiting
room wouldn't prevent it.

I don't remember the trip across town. I walked
through the theatergoers, hurrying to check out the

name Eileen had mumbled. Elusive memories of an old court case stirred but remained out of reach.

A thin crack of light seeped from beneath the office door. I thought, Please, no more surprises, and quietly stuck a key in the lock.

A worried voice called, "Who's there?"

"Jona, is that you? Why are you still here? It's after seven. You should have gone home hours ago."

Jona rushed out. The employer/employee barrier crumbled, and she hugged me. "I was worried; I knew you'd come back here so I decided to wait. How is Eileen?"

It was a question I was tired of hearing and even more tired of answering, but Jona had been with us since the beginning; she deserved an answer. I gave her a brief report, then asked, "Where are Eileen's old case notes?"

"How old?"

"Nine, maybe ten years."

Her forehead crinkled. "Ten years. That would be before you and Eileen started to work together. If they're in this office, they're in the back of the file room. It shouldn't be too difficult to locate them." She started to walk down the hallway to the storeroom, and I followed behind. "What are you looking for?"

"Eileen mentioned a name that sounded vaguely familiar. I think it's from one of her old cases. Rudy MacIntyre. Does that sound familiar to you?"

Jona stopped so abruptly that I walked into her. Her face was ashen. "He was here. Last week. He was here."

"Are you sure it was MacIntyre? When was he here?"

Jona nodded. "I'm positive. It was Thursday. I spent the day at the switchboard because no one else was available. Remember?"

I remembered. Last Thursday hadn't been one of my better days. I'd been angry, had bitched to Eileen about my work being ignored, and had spent the rest of the day sulking in my office. "Tell me what happened."

"He didn't have an appointment. He walked in and demanded to see Eileen. He looked like he was auditioning for a James Dean movie. Leather jacket, T-shirt, cigarette hanging from his mouth. He was rude too. Eileen refused to see him."

"What did he do?"

"He said he'd come back when Eileen wasn't so busy. Then he left."

"Did Eileen say anything to you?"

"Not right away. She came out later to pick up some messages and said she wouldn't take any calls from him. Eileen wasn't very concerned, so I forgot about him. Do you think MacIntyre could have..."

Jona couldn't finish the sentence. I shrugged. "I don't know. Let's get those files, maybe I'll find something in them."

The small, windowless storeroom was lined with metal shelves stretching from floor to ceiling. Almost every inch of the shelves was covered with cardboard storage boxes. Visions of an endless evening of peeking into dusty boxes struck, and I groaned.

Jona laughed. "It's not that bad. These are stacked in chronological order." She located the right box without any trouble; we dusted it off and carted it back to my office. I sent Jona home and settled down with coffee and cigarettes for an evening of reading.

I STARED at the blue lines of the legal pad. They were still empty, waiting for the notes I had confidently prepared to take. The battered cardboard storage box sat on the floor next to my desk, its contents spread across the carpet.

My only problem was that I didn't know which file to pick up first, so I scanned all of them, searching for MacIntyre's name. I read about everything—except Rudy MacIntyre. My sister was a compulsive note taker. Notes about meetings, notes about telephone calls, notes of tasks to be accomplished—each one carefully ticked off after completion—and notes about cases. Notes on yellow legal pads, notes on cocktail napkins, notes written in blue ink, notes written in pencil, notes blurred and faded.

I lit a cigarette and stared at the piles of notes. When the cigarette had burned down to the filter, I reluctantly crept through the dark conference room to Eileen's office. I took a deep breath, flicked the lights on, and hurried across the floor.

Telling myself they didn't exist, I skirted around the stains on the carpet and gingerly prodded the rubble. The telephone rang. Amazed that it still worked, I picked up the receiver.

Don's quiet voice greeted me. I held my breath, waiting for the bad news. "Nothing's changed. The doctors said I should go home. Why don't you come to the house? Sandy could use a visit from her favorite aunt; she doesn't understand what's going on. We'll have dinner."

I wasn't hungry, but I agreed. I would have agreed to anything that gave me a reason to leave.

DON ANSWERED THE DOOR. Sandy, my four-year-old niece, was perched on his shoulders. She shouted "Aunt B!" dove into my arms, and looked over my shoulder for her mother. Before she could ask any questions, I hugged her. "Hey, I'm hungry. What's for dinner? I don't smell anything cooking."

Sandy smiled and giggled. "Daddy let me order. We're having moo shu pancakes. Do you want moo shu pancakes?"

Don pushed us toward the kitchen. "Everybody wants moo shu pancakes. Let's get the table set, the food will be here soon."

Sandy took charge; I sat, safely out of the way, to watch. She was an enthusiastic, but inaccurate, table setter. I retrieved errant silverware from the floor and smoked a cigarette. Not wanting to upset the delicate balance of our fantasy, I didn't ask about Eileen.

The bubble around our pretense lasted through dinner, into the fortune cookies. Sandy, who loves the cookies with the tiny notes inside, distributed them and waited for us to read the magical messages. I was last. I crumpled the cookie, unfolded the note, and read, "You will meet much sorrow on the way to happiness." I lit a cigarette and held the match to the fortune.

Don watched as I dropped the burning embers into an ashtray. He sighed. "It's been a long day." Sandy, sensing that boring adult conversation was about to begin, skipped off to strew toys around the living room. "Dr. Mabe told me to come home. There isn't anything I can do at the hospital. They won't let me spend much time with Eileen."

"What about Eileen's eyes? Did they tell you anything about them?" Don shrugged and started to clear dishes of congealed leftovers from the table. I changed the subject. "Was Eileen worried about anything lately?"

Don scraped dishes and ran water into the dishpan. "She was preoccupied. Typical Eileen, you know how she gets. Distant, difficult to talk to. She said work was hectic and nothing was wrong."

"Do you mind if I poke around in the desk?" Don, a pilot, rarely brought work home from the cockpit. The desk would be crammed with Eileen's papers, and I was hoping MacIntyre's file would be among them.

Don dropped a plate into the dishpan and turned to look at me. "What do you think you'll find in there?"

One part of my mind was amazed that we could be speaking in such matter-of-fact voices, another part was horrified. I didn't stop to think about the contrast. "Eileen came to the surface for a few moments this afternoon. She recognized me and mumbled a name. I think Eileen brought the files home."

"What did your cop friend say?"

"Nothing. I didn't tell him." Don raised an eyebrow. He and Eileen were a perfect couple, still believing in Superman's credo.

Don tried to interrupt but I wouldn't let him. "The investigation is going to get a lot of publicity today. A more gruesome story will take its place tomorrow and the reporters will go away. After a few days the cops will disappear too. They'll get reassigned until only two or three overworked detectives follow up on bad leads. No one else cares enough to keep at it."

Don turned away and addressed the greasy water in the sink. "I care too. Do what you have to do. You know where the desk is. Take your time. I'm going to give Sandy a bath and put her to bed."

The battered desk was in the living room taking up an entire corner. I sat behind the huge desk and blinked back a few tears before opening the drawers. MacIntyre's file was in the center drawer, on top of everything else. Easily accessible to a worried person who wanted to review its contents. I pulled the file and took it back to the kitchen.

Eileen's handwriting hadn't changed much during the past ten years. It was a little less cramped, a little less rushed, but distinctively Eileen's. I skimmed the notes and closed the file; my memories of Rudy MacIntyre were returning.

Don's quiet voice interrupted my musing. "Sandy wants to say good-night to you." I tucked the file under my arm and went off to my niece's bedroom. After a story, a good-night kiss and hug, I returned to the kitchen. Don was sitting at the table, waiting.

I tossed the file on the table and made coffee. Don looked at the label and asked, "Who's MacIntyre?"

"That was the last case Eileen prosecuted before she left the district attorney's office. I should have remembered the name. It was an ugly case; Eileen won. MacIntyre accused her of ruining his life and threatened to kill her."

"I don't think Eileen ever mentioned him. What did he do?"

"MacIntyre's wife wanted a divorce, he didn't. He put a little bomb together and hid it under the dashboard of her car. That's a great place for a bomb; the full force of the explosion hits the people in the front seat. She was killed instantly. MacIntyre claimed he was framed. The jury didn't believe him."

"Why would you suspect him? Isn't he in jail?"

"It was a manslaughter conviction—ten to fifteen years. He's out. MacIntyre appeared at the office last week, demanding to see Eileen. She refused. A few days later a bomb goes off in her office. I'd say that makes him my number one suspect."

"She never said anything." Don stopped playing with the coffee mug and looked at me. "What are you going to do?"

"Find him."

SEVEN

I MADE MY WAY to WARM and ran up the stairs, taking them two at a time. Light shone through the frosted glass of the door, backlighting the dark letters on the door. The M was gone from the logo, proclaiming the office as the home of WAR. Accidental or intentional?

I pushed the door open without knocking and walked in, ready to do battle. Roz and Collier Whitehead were sitting at the table, heads bent over the papers spread across its surface. My unannounced entrance startled them.

"Sorry to interrupt." I walked closer, trying to get a peek at their papers.

Roz didn't hide her annoyance. She snapped, "Grant's not here."

"Grant left me a few messages, I haven't been able to get back to him. I was hoping he might still be here. Is he coming back? I can wait."

"He's not here. Don't bother to wait, I don't know when he's coming back. I'll tell him you were here."

I was almost close enough to decipher the writing. Baldhead noticed. He covered the pages and asked, "Do you want something? We're quite busy and don't have time to worry because you can't find your boyfriend."

"What?" Roz and I spoke at the same time, using the same tone of disbelief. I closed my mouth and let

Roz chew him out. "Don't be stupid, Collier. She missed our meeting last night. Grant was calling to find out if she was going to show up tomorrow. We need bodies, even if they aren't committed."

Tomorrow? The demonstration at the fur store—forgotten in the turmoil with Eileen. I recovered by the time Roz turned to me. "Are you still planning to join us tomorrow? Or is your schedule too crowded with other social events?"

I slid into the chair next to Whitehead. "My purpose in joining this group was to work with you to end animal exploitation. I didn't come to fight. Why are you so hostile?"

Roz blushed but didn't apologize. "We are not being hostile. We are being careful. We are fighting a war. Caution in the selection of new recruits is necessary."

They looked ready to toss me out. I gambled and asked, "What do I have to do to prove I'm serious? Blow something up?"

Silence.

"I'll be at the demonstration tomorrow. I'll also be waiting for you to decide how I can prove myself."

It's easy to be gawky when you're an inch under six feet tall. People are never surprised by a sudden lack of coordination. I stood up and awkwardly swung my elbows out, managing to sweep Whitehead's papers from the table.

We dove for them, almost knocking our heads together in the rush to be first. I won the race. Whitehead silently held out his hand. Apologizing for my clumsiness, I gave him the papers—they were blueprints—and left.

If it had been a normal evening I would have gone home to bed, but this wasn't a normal evening. I went to the hospital.

A NURSE STOPPED ME at the ICU entrance. "You can't go in now, the doctors are in with her." I protested but she wasn't swayed by my appeal. "You'll have to wait in the lounge. I'll call you when you can see her."

I followed instructions without raising a fuss and went to the lounge, expecting to find those three women sitting in the corner. To my relief, the room was empty. I flipped through a six-month-old magazine and smoked half a dozen cigarettes.

The door squeaked open. I looked up, hoping it was the nurse. Brad walked in and smiled. "Hi, Babe, the nurse told me you were here. What are you doing here? Don't you ever sleep?"

Brad's eyes were bloodshot, his clothes rumpled and wrinkled. "You look like you could use a little sleep yourself."

He loosened his tie and sat down. "I stopped for one last visit with Eileen before leaving. The overnight crew is all set and in place. I called—"

"Stop. You wouldn't be leaving if you didn't have good people assigned. Did anything exciting happen around here today?"

He yawned. "Not a damn thing. How 'bout you?"

Brad continued to yawn while I told him about my trip to WARM's office. I said, "When I walked in, Roz and Whitehead were studying the blueprints of a building on New Street. Whitehead made a point of covering them up." I grinned. "But I managed to knock them off the table. Do you know where New Street is?"

"Nope." He yawned again. "Look, Babe, I'd love to talk geography with you but I'm ready to pass out. I need two or three weeks' sleep. What about you, are you going home?"

"Not yet, I'm going to stay here. The nurse said I could see Eileen." I stood and pulled Brad to his feet. "Go home: that's an order. Don't worry about me, I won't stay long. I'll leave as soon as the nurses throw me out."

Brad wasn't convinced but he had put in too many hours to argue. I pushed him to the door and watched him shuffle down the corridor before turning back to the empty lounge. What would I do without Brad? Minutes after he left, a nurse appeared in the doorway and motioned for me to follow her. I spent the night in the chair next to Eileen's bed, her hand resting in mine. Thinking about the years we'd been working together. A light touch on my shoulder jolted me awake.

Dr. Mabe's fresh, smiling face greeted me. "Good morning. You must have been exceptionally charming to the nursing staff, they didn't want to wake you."

"Brad's the one who's been charming. I'm riding on his coattails." I stretched and looked at my watch. Six-fifteen. A hundred stiff muscles complained about spending the night in a chair; I stretched again and glanced at the bed. Eileen hadn't reacted to our voices. I looked away and asked, "How is she?"

"Better." Dr. Mabe examined my face. "When was the last time you ate? Let's go to the cafeteria. I promise to answer your questions if you promise to eat—I don't want both of you as patients at the same time.''

Without arguing, I followed her to the cafeteria. My stomach agreed with her prescription; even the hospital food smelled appetizing. Dr. Mabe drank two cups of tea and smoked three cigarettes while I devoured a full breakfast. When my plate was empty, I sat back and took one of the doctor's cigarettes. "Okay, Doc, keep your part of the bargain. Tell me about Eileen. The doctors I saw last night couldn't answer my questions."

"It's too early for answers. Apparently the bomb exploded—"

"You told me that already. What else do you know?"

"Nothing." Dr. Mabe stabbed her cigarette out in the tin ashtray. "Eileen's alive. That's it. Now, take my good advice. You look like hell. Go home. Go to sleep."

We both knew her advice was useless. I wasn't going to heed it.

IT WAS A LOVELY DAY for a demonstration. The air was hot, hinting at the humid summer that was approaching. Despite Brad's warnings, I left my gun and the concealing jacket in the office. I rolled the sleeves of my blouse over and winced as I absentmindedly rubbed the burn mark on my forearm. The itchy scab had fallen off, exposing a slash of tender skin. I gently massaged the mark, hoping its ragged edges would meld into my arm without leaving a scar.

Royal blue police barricades, a perfect match of the brilliant sky, had been erected along the curb, keeping the crowd away from the fur store, on the opposite side of the street. It wasn't much of a crowd; cops outnumbered protestors two to one.

The cops were standing in small groups, gossiping, laughing, and ignoring the gathering protestors. Inside the enclosure, Roz and several helpers bustled around piling stacks of literature on sagging card tables. I ducked under the sawhorses to join them. A woman cradling a load of posters in her arms greeted me. The woman, a member of the gaggle at the WARM seminar, smiled and offered me a poster.

FUR KILLS—STAY WARM WITH CLOTH or SAY NO TO FURS—DRESS WITH HEART, NOT SKINS. Trying to think of an acceptable reason for refusing both, I hesitated. A voice behind me said snidely, "So you decided to show up. You made quite an interesting challenge last night."

"Rosalynn." I turned and smiled. The image of Eileen in the hospital bed kept me from slapping the woman's face. "Are we going to work together, or would you rather fight it out right here in the middle of Fifth Avenue?"

Grant appeared in time to overhear the exchange. He put his hand on my bare elbow and squeezed gently. I tried to move away, but the hand followed. Grant laughed. "Can you two wait fifteen or twenty minutes before you start slugging it out? The television crews aren't here yet. They would hate to miss action shots of two sexy ladies brawling in the center of Fifth Avenue." He stopped smiling. "What's wrong here?"

Roz was under too much pressure to be teased into a good mood. She yelled, "Where have you been? The cops won't let us across the street. How are we going to stop the fur show if we can't keep people out of the store? You have to do something."

Roz led Grant away. He winked at me over his shoulder, letting me know he was firmly in control. They were quickly embroiled in a discussion with a white-shirted police commander. I watched for a few minutes but soon lost interest.

The cops-to-crowd ratio slowly dropped until, with five minutes to spare, the crowd was finally larger than the guards. Sensing the change in size and tempo, the police took up their positions: shoulder to shoulder, feet apart, backs to the street. Impassive police faces watched us. We watched them. A dozen guards marched out of Renkel's and lined up in front of the store. They folded their arms across their chests and stared. Stone-cold disapproval rocketed across the street.

High noon. Almost a hundred people had gathered behind the wooden barricades. Some held signs, some waited patiently, others attempted to thrust leaflets into the hands of the harried passersby. Most refused the flyers, a few cursed the impassable sidewalk and tossed the papers to the ground.

"Fur kills! Fur kills!" The low chant rumbled from the center of the group and swelled to an angry roar. Television cameras whirred.

The mob surged forward. The cops held their ground. My stomach fell in a slow-motion, nervous roll. I was solidly wedged in the middle of the demonstrators. I tried to drop back to the fringe but couldn't move—the bodies were packed together tighter than a rush hour F train.

Another surge against the barriers ended in another standoff. The cries of "Fur kills!" were replaced by a soft muttering from the rear. "Cross the street. Cross the street. Cross the street."

Across the street, limousines arrived and paused to discharge passengers. Jeers and catcalls greeted everyone who stepped out. The crowd swelled through the police line and flowed over the barricades into the center of Fifth Avenue. Traffic stopped. Horns and curses filled the air.

The melee began without warning. From the corner of my eye I saw an arm whipping forward in a clumsy pitching motion. I turned—Amy, resplendent in a tie-dyed blouse, stood on my left. She caught my eye and grinned. Her hand dipped into the fringed bag hanging from her shoulder and came out holding a chunk of concrete. Following another angelic grin, she tossed the rock at a policeman. Her windup was awkward but she threw a perfect strike.

The jagged hunk of concrete bounced off the face of a cop and fell to the ground. The enraged cop resettled his cap on his head and wiped his cheek. He looked at the red droplets of blood on his fingers and bellowed, "Get her! Arrest her!" He charged, twirling his nightclub overhead. His uniformed colleagues followed, indiscriminately slashing at anyone who impeded their chase.

A vital brain cell stopped functioning. In the few seconds it took for me to realize that the cop was pointing at me, he flew across the pavement, pushing bodies from his path. Two steps and he was at my side, nightstick poised to strike. I raised my arm to protect my face and tried to backpedal out of reach. There wasn't any room to maneuver. The blow landed squarely on the raw skin on my forearm, and pain ricocheted through my body. My knees buckled. I headed to the ground.

EIGHT

A HAND, pinkie and ring fingers missing, yanked me to my feet. I grabbed hold and lowered my head, blindly following Grant's lead. We scrambled through the swirling bodies to the clear sidewalk beyond the barricades. The cop followed, shouting, "Stop her! Get her!" Several blue shirts joined the chase, desperately trying to get their nightsticks on me. My fellow protestors closed around them, blocking the path. The cops responded by swinging their clubs at anyone in their way.

We broke free and stumbled around to the corner to Fifty-second Street. Grant shoved me into an alcove next to a bookstore and pushed me back into the shadows. He hugged me and nuzzled my ear. I barely heard the word he breathed in my ear: "Cop."

I buried my face in Grant's chest and listened to the click of the cop's shoes on the pavement. The footsteps stopped. The cop hesitated, then stepped into the dark niche for a closer look at us. Wrapping my arms around Grant's shoulders, I murmured "Be convincing," and kissed him. Warning sirens sounded, telling me of the mistake I was making. I ignored them. The cop lost interest and walked away. We didn't notice.

"Wow." Grant moved back a half step, and I looked down at my feet so I wouldn't have to look in his eyes. Grant gently tilted my head back. "I think that cop is coming back."

We couldn't take any chances—I was a fugitive. We kissed again.

The warnings were too strong to ignore this time. I reluctantly pushed him away and caught my breath. "Hey, I think we're safe now."

"Are we?" I forced my lips away from his face. I wouldn't be able to resist for long if I continued to stare into those blue eyes. "We shouldn't rush out of our cozy hiding place. Cops might be lurking around the corner, waiting to pounce on you."

Grant leaned closer. I backed away. "You're the only one waiting to pounce. Let's get out of here."

"Your place or mine?"

The magic evaporated; I wanted to get out of the alley. I skipped over Grant's leering invitation without comment. "Shouldn't we pick up the pieces, see who needs bail money?"

Grant shook his head. "We can't take the chance. Those cops might recognize you—you don't exactly blend into the crowd. What'd you do to get that cop so mad?"

"Nothing—"

"Nothing? That pig was swinging for your head. If you hadn't stuck your arm up, you'd be in the emergency room waiting for stitches in your scalp. Let me see." He grabbed my arm. "You're going to have an outstanding black-and-blue mark."

I winced and gingerly removed his hand. "The only thing I did wrong was to stand next to Amy. She flung a hunk of concrete at that cop. Of course, since I'm about six inches taller than her and—as you so kindly

pointed out—stand out in a crowd, he decided I was
the troublemaker." I folded my arms across my chest,
carefully keeping the bruised one away from Grant.
"Was Amy ad-libbing, or was starting a riot part of
the game plan? It would have been nice if someone
had warned me."

"We didn't know how much we could tell you. Then
you missed the meeting—"

"Next time I miss a meeting, I'll get a note from my
mother. Roz already jumped down my throat because
I don't spend every minute of my life at WARM headquarters. What's her problem?"

"Roz always worries that every newcomer is a government spy. Don't worry, she'll loosen up—unless
you *are* a cop."

"You guys are lunatics. A cop just tried to take my
head off and you're asking me if I'm a cop! I don't
know if I can be part of WARM, I'm not crazy
enough. I'm also tired of trying to convince you and
Roz that I have talent you could use." I moved to push
past him.

"Wait." He grabbed my arm again—my poor arm
was going to be black and blue from all this abuse—
and whispered, "I don't think you're a cop. Cops
don't kiss like this..."

I RETURNED to my office and settled behind my desk
to think and rub an ice pack against my bruised arm.
The stack of files on my desk was reaching new
heights; I couldn't put the work off any longer. There
was too much to do. My work, Eileen's work, Rudy
MacIntyre, Faradeux.... Once again, I had under-

estimated the amount of time a case would take. It was time to drop something before everything crumbled.

Hurley Blake. I wrote his name on a pad, stared at it for a few minutes, then slowly drew a thick black mark through it. Someone else would have to fight Wina's battle.

As if guided by ESP, Wina Blake burst into my office. Jona followed behind apologizing. "Blaine, I'm sorry. I tried to stop her."

"Tell her to leave me be. I got to talk to you." The girl was panting; sweat rolled down her face. She threw herself into a chair and wiped her forehead with a ragged tissue.

Storming offices was a tactic I had used more than once so it was difficult for me to reprimand her. I tried. "It's our custom to expect people to make appointments, not just run in without warning. What's wrong?"

"You keep that cop away from my grammie. He bother her again, I'm gonna get myself another gun and stop him."

"Calm down. Who's been bothering your grandmother?"

"That cop who was after my daddy came to the house. I'm not going to let him hurt Grammie. She's old, she been sick ever since . . . ever since the fire. He do it again, I'll kill him."

"I can't help you if you don't stop threatening to kill people and tell me everything that happened. Who is this cop? What did he want?"

"Don't know his name. Said he was looking for evidence." The words were spit from her mouth like curses. "Grammie wouldn't let him in, said he didn't have papers. She meant a search warrant. Mother-fucker better keep away.''

My old friend, guilt, stirred. Suspicion followed close behind. The anonymous cop had to be Tony Parker, and if Parker was searching for Hurley Blake's papers, I had to see them before he did. "I want you to go home. If any cops show up, call me immediately. Don't let them in unless they have a search warrant. I'll stop by your house tonight to talk to your grandmother.''

Wina surprised me. She agreed and left without arguing. I shook my head—so much for giving up on Hurley Blake—and concentrated on the work on my desk without much success. I decided to call it a day before any more surprise visitors stormed my offices.

I hurried down Seventh Avenue, turned the corner to Barrow Street, and slowed my quick pace. There was a man sitting on the front steps of my house. Brad's warnings immediately came to mind but it was too late to follow his advice about carrying my gun. The man spotted me and got to his feet.

It was Dennis Halstead. A grin of relief crossed my face. Given a choice, I always prefer to find an FBI man sitting on my front steps instead of a mad bomber. Halstead misinterpreted my smile; he thought it was meant to welcome him.

"Blaine, don't say anything. I came to apologize for acting like a swine the other day. I called your office; Jona told me you had already left. I decided to wait here." Dennis was nervous, and he rushed on. "Can we go inside? Your neighbor across the street keeps peering out from behind her curtains. She's probably getting ready to call the cops.''

I glanced across the street. The drapery over the living room windows moved slightly. I groaned. "Ida means well, but she can be a pain in the ass. I'm surprised she hasn't called the cops. Come in, let's get out of her sight." The telephone started to ring seconds after we stepped inside. Before the door finished closing, I dumped my briefcase on the floor and ran down the hallway to answer the phone. Dennis wandered into the living room.

Of course, it was Ida. "I hope I'm not interrupting anything important. I called to thank you for taking the time to get Mikey's birdseed. Mikey just loves it." She chattered on while I kicked off my heels, rubbed my aching feet, and waited patiently for an opening. When Ida started on a second round of thank-you's, I politely ended the conversation. Dennis was too engrossed in studying the picture in his hands to hear me come into the living room. It was a picture from the mantel, a picture of my husband taken on our wedding day. A floorboard creaked underfoot. Dennis gently returned the picture to its place on the mantel. He stared at it and said, "You know, I still miss him."

"So do I." My eyes filled with tears. I blinked and roughly cleared my throat. "Do you want coffee or something cold to drink?"

"No, maybe later." Dennis loosened his silk tie and pulled an envelope from his pocket. He turned it over in his hands, not sure if he should part with it. "I called some people who owe me favors. This is a copy of the lab report about the bomb."

He thrust the envelope at me, getting rid of it before he changed his mind. Dennis stuck his hands in his trouser pockets and paced the room. I ripped the envelope open and scanned the report.

After one quick reading, I put the report aside and asked, "What's C-4? I don't remember that from chemistry classes."

"Composition four. It's something you never studied in chemistry." Dennis continued lecturing as he paced. "It's the most popular plastic explosive around these days. C-4 is handy, it's soft, and can be molded to fit anywhere."

"You obviously know this stuff." I folded the papers and shoved them back in the envelope. "Why don't you tell me about it? I can read the report later."

Dennis took off the glasses he had recently started wearing and wiped the lenses. I lit a cigarette and watched. Was he regretting the impulsive action that brought him to my stairs?

Dennis gazed out the window and spoke rapidly, not giving me any opportunity to ask questions. "The bomb was in a small package, about the size of a paperback book. The C-4 was used as the main explosive charge. They used a wristwatch for the timer. The box was packed with metal fragments, nails, bolts. It's called people's shrapnel—the purpose is to cause as much injury as possible. We recovered pieces of the watch, fragments of the box and the paper it was wrapped in." He shrugged. "Maybe we'll get lucky and trace something back to the store where it was purchased. Or maybe we'll come up with a suspect and find comparable materials in his apartment."

"Or maybe we'll win the lottery and retire."

"Actually, reconstructing the bomb is quite helpful to an investigation. Most people think everything is incinerated by the blast. That's not true. We learned a lot about your bomber. He's either an old-timer who's out of practice or a newcomer with old reference books. The bomb was a very simple design from an old sixties terrorist manual. It's a very unreliable bomb. Eileen tossed the package on her desk and probably jarred something loose." He took a deep breath and said, "That's about all I can tell you."

"Where do people get this C-4?"

Halstead laughed. "This is New York City. If you have enough money, you can get anything, even plastic explosives."

"I know that. Where do these explosives come from, some foreign country?"

"The army." He waited for my reaction, knowing what it would be.

"You're kidding! The C-4 came from the army? Our army?"

"I'm not saying the explosives in your sister's bomb definitely came from the army. But odds are that the C-4 came from Fort Dix or one of the other East Coast bases. Each year, millions of dollars of weapons and explosives disappear from military installations. It turns up here, in Philadelphia, or any large city. The army doesn't like to talk about this little problem. That's all I can tell you. How about dinner?"

His quick shift surprised me. I recovered and shook my head. "Sorry, I can't."

"You could have pretended to think about it before turning me down." He nodded at Jeff's picture. "You can't stay in mourning forever. It's time to get on with your life."

"Don't worry, I'm not sitting around in the dark, worshiping Jeff's memory. I'm certainly not wasting away." The crestfallen look on Dennis's face made me reconsider the angry words I was preparing to fling at him. "Damn it, Dennis, why do we always scream at each other?" Dennis quietly pointed out that I was the one doing the screaming. I ignored him. "I was going to say that I have to work tonight and suggest another evening. What are you doing tomorrow?"

Dennis tried to act cool, but I knew he was pleased. I walked him to the door and watched him amble down the street. My stomach tightened. I wasn't sure if the feeling was fueled by pleasure or dread.

NINE

WINA AND GRAMMIE BLAKE lived on Avenue B, five blocks south of the remains of Hurley Blake's bodega. The apartment building was a typical Alphabet City tenement: a run-down, five-story brick walk-up in the middle of a long block filled with similarly disintegrating buildings.

Shattered locks hung uselessly from the outer door, which swung open under my light touch. I stepped over the Chinese menus scattered across the doorstep and walked inside. The stench of urine in the lobby stung my eyes. I gagged and sprinted up the stairs, hurrying past the dark corners of the landings.

Locating Wina's apartment was easy—my ears followed the music booming down the hallway. Grammie must be deaf.

I pounded on the door to 5-G and waited. The guitar solo abruptly ended, locks tumbled, and the battered metal door opened. Wina's sullen face greeted me. She let me into the dim apartment and reengaged the locks.

"Grammie went to a church meeting. You can wait in the sitting room till she comes back."

Wina began to lead me down a hallway, but I stopped her. "Which room was your father's? I'd like to look around, see if I can find anything that would interest the cops."

Wina's thumb gestured at a closed door. "It's there. You want help?" She was uneasy about leaving me alone but too frightened to walk into his room. An eyelid twitched from the strain of acting cool.

"No, we'd only trip over each other." Help was the last thing I wanted. I waited, hand on the doorknob, while Wina decided if she could enter the room.

"Yeah, okay. I got to study." She scurried down the hallway to her bedroom and slammed the door.

Hurley Blake's room had been transformed into a shrine. I recognized the signs—I was an expert at making shrines for dead loved ones. Every trace of Hurley's personality had been removed, the room sterilized by his mother's attempts to polish grief from her system.

I prowled the room, randomly opening drawers and pawing through the contents. Grammie's cleaning had been thorough; the drawers and file cabinets were empty. No notebooks, no journals, no papers. I dropped to my knees to check under the bed. Nothing, not even a dust ball, was in sight.

A woman's stern voice sounded behind me. "What are you doing? Get out from there and explain yourself."

I wiggled from beneath the bed and stood up to face an irate elderly woman. She looked at my tight jeans and tighter blouse with distaste. "Who let you in here? If you have papers from the court saying you can come into my home without permission, give them to me."

Wina rushed in. "Grammie, she's no cop. She's the investigator I told you about."

The grandmother's wrath swung to the teenager. "Edwina, why don't you listen to me? I told you to let it go. Your daddy's gone, all we can do is pray for his immortal soul. Now go back to your studying. This is grown-up business."

Wina disappeared without a comment. Grammie turned back to me, her temper unabated. "People today don't respect anything. You come into my home, dressed like a whore, and search through my son's belongings without my knowledge or permission."

"Mrs. Blake, please forgive me." I ignored the comment about my clothes; I had spent a lot of time choosing an outfit appropriate for an evening of barhopping. "I assumed Wina had your permission to invite me here. You should also understand that Wina asked me to come here because she is concerned about your welfare. I am sorry if I offended you."

"Leave my house. Please do not come back or try to see my granddaughter. We're poor people. You have nothing to gain from us."

I didn't attempt to argue or explain, the woman was too irate to listen. Ignoring the faint tremors of guilt in my stomach, I left the apartment and walked down the stairs. Once outside, I stood in the shadow of the building to smoke a cigarette and psyche myself for the rest of the evening.

Wina rushed through the door, spotted me, and stopped. "Grammie told me to stop you," she puffed. The kid was cutting too many phys ed classes. "You gotta come back. She wants to talk to you about Daddy."

"Does your grandmother really want to talk, or does she want to lecture me?"

"Naw, Grammie's okay. She's just worried. You gotta come back."

I sighed and flicked the cigarette into the street. It bounced off a parked car into a storm drain. Wina ran up the stairs, her dreadlocks bouncing against her shoulders as I trudged behind. Only curiosity about Parker's interest in Hurley Blake propelled me back to the airless apartment.

Wina led me down the familiar hallway to the living room, then disappeared. I hesitated in the doorway and looked around. Furniture common to every grandmother in the country filled the room. Wing chairs and sofa, upholstered in matching flowery material, took up most of the space. The decor was completed by a television set with pictures of children and grandchildren in gilded frames standing in orderly rows on top, and a low, freshly polished coffee table covered with religious magazines.

Grammie had assumed a regal pose on the sofa. She patted the flowered cushions and waved a hand over the gleaming tea service on the table. "Come sit here beside me. I made tea."

Dr. Jekyll and Grammie Hyde. I sat, but refused the tea. Grammie filled a cup, added sugar and milk, and delicately tasted the brew. I watched and longed for another cigarette.

"Miss Stewart, please accept my apology. The good Lord saw fit to bless me with a terrible temper. I was rude and should have given you the opportunity to explain. Do forgive me. Edwina told me you are the person who attempted to save my son's life. I have prayed for you. It was a brave thing you did."

Brushing her thank-you's aside, I jumped back into business. "I promised Wina I would investigate the cause of the fire. She seemed anxious for my help."

"Thank you for your concern for my granddaughter. However, there is nothing for you to investigate. I am completely satisfied with the police report. The fire was an accident. All you can do is pray for Hurley's soul."

Time for a tea break. I filled a cup and sipped the tepid brew. "Wina told me a policeman came here this afternoon. What can you tell me about the papers he was trying to find?"

"Hurley was not a saint." She balanced the cup and saucer in one hand and used the other to wipe a handkerchief across her eyes. "He tried to be a good man but he was weak. He gave in to temptation. My son didn't have the courage to mend his ways. It was easier for him to take money from innocent people and pass it to the Devil than to pray to Almighty God for the strength to resist. Miss Stewart, there are no papers. I burned everything, every scrap of paper, and prayed for my son's immortal soul as the flames consumed the evilness. I prayed that his soul would be delivered from the everlasting fires of Hell."

I put the cup down with more force than intended. The clatter interrupted Grammie's sermonizing. Taking advantage of the pause, I gently asked, "What evil was your son involved in?"

The elderly woman responded by reciting Bible passages about fire and hot tar raining down on Sodom and Gomorrah until I cut in. "The cop who was pounding on your door this afternoon wanted more than Scripture quotes. He'll be back. He'll keep coming back until he finds those papers and he won't believe you burned them. I might be able to convince

him to stay away but I need to know what he's looking for.''

Grammie stared over my head at the crucifix on the
wall and mumbled, ''The Lord is my Shepherd . . .''

The interview was over. Grammie didn't notice me
leave, she was busy praying. I quietly walked past the
closed door of Wina's bedroom and left the apartment.

THE EASIEST WAY to find a missing person is to look in
his old hangouts. Old habits, especially bad ones,
don't change. People always find their way back to
their favorite haunts. Eileen's notes, although dated,
contained volumes of information about Rudy
MacIntyre and his habits.

MacIntyre had favored dingy bars tucked into the
twisting streets of lower Manhattan. Those bars were
still there and I was betting I'd find him in one of
them.

The bars MacIntyre frequented were all alike: loud,
smoky, and crowded. I made the rounds of every dive
in lower Manhattan, ordering bottles of beer that I left
untasted, rebuffing the passes of scuzzy barmates, and
asking questions. No one admitted to knowing Rudy
MacIntyre. Jona's vague description didn't help—
everyone, male or female, was dressed like James
Dean. Black leather was the haute couture.

Billy's Brewhouse was my last stop. Tired, cranky,
and ready for bed, I promised this would definitely be
my last stop for the evening and shoved the door open.
Billy's wasn't like the other bars. It wasn't smoke-
filled, it wasn't loud, and it wasn't crowded.

Two customers, bulky men in black leather jackets, were sitting at the bar, steps away from the door. Neither one looked up from his beer mug when I walked past—so much for my carefully chosen outfit. A half dozen people were on a small stage in the back of the bar, unpacking instruments, checking microphones, and tripping over each other.

I settled on an empty stool midway down the bar and waited. The bartender glanced at me and finished the story he was telling to a waitress before ambling my way. I asked for a beer—this wasn't the type of place to ask for a seltzer. He nodded and walked away without answering. Billy's wouldn't win any awards for outstanding service.

The bartender pulled a bottle from a cooler, strolled back, and set the bottle down in front of me. "We're out of that fancy stuff you wanted. Will this do?"

"A beer's a beer. Long as I get a buzz, I don't care what you put in front of me."

He popped the lid off and tried to look interested, instinctively following the unwritten bartender's rule that sympathy increases the tip. "Bad day?"

"The usual—it sucked. How 'bout you?"

"Every day sucks. This city sucks. This job sucks. Just wait till the band starts, they really suck." He pulled another beer from beneath the counter and came back. After taking a long swallow he said, "This beer sucks too. Least I don't have to pay for it."

I tried to start a conversation before the band finished tuning up. After a few minutes commiserating about hard living in the city, I asked, "Hey, do you know a guy named Rudy? Last name's Irish.

MacSomething. MacIntyre—that's it. Rudy Mac-
Intyre. Do you know him?"

"Nope." The strain of being friendly had exhausted the bartender. He tossed the bottle into the
trash and joined the men at the end of the bar. I played
with the beer bottle and watched the band set up,
wondering if I was losing my touch. I couldn't bully a
grandmother into giving me information and I
couldn't make friends with a bored bartender.

The band lashed into their set, and the grating noise
made me flinch. The bartender was right—they were
bad. When the bartender wandered back, he had to
shout to be heard over the band's clamor.

"What'd you say that guy's name was? You know,
that guy you're looking for."

"MacIntyre. He used to hang here. Friend of mine
said to look him up if I ever got down here."

The bartender nodded and went back to his buddies. A prickly sensation moved along the back of my
neck. He was reporting on our conversation. I lit a
cigarette and pretended to be fascinated by the band.

The conference ended. My go-between bartender
returned and resumed shouting across the bar.
"Who's the friend that told you Rudy hangs here?"

The band stopped bashing their guitars and hopped
off the stage to take a break; I didn't have to shout my
insulting response. I blew smoke into his face and said,
"I'm tired of this game. I ain't playing with you no
more. Tell your pals to drag their sorry butts down
here and talk to me themselves. I ain't talking to you
unless I want more beer."

"Bitch."

His buddies didn't like my answer. They slid off the stools and marched around the corner of the bar. Twin linebackers in leather jackets, close-cropped hair, tight blue jeans, and white T-shirts under their jackets. My stomach tightened. I calmly grabbed the bottle, ready to use it as a weapon if necessary.

The larger man stationed himself on my left, the other on my right. The guy on my right was the designated spokesman. He leaned closer and breathed beer into my face. "Having a good time, honey?"

I studied my reflection in his mirrored sunglasses; I didn't look nervous. "Reasonable. How about you boys? Are you having a good time? Hey, are you guys brothers? You know, you look alike. If your buddy shaved his beard, you'd look like twins." I laughed. "But people tell you that all the time, don't they?"

He didn't answer. I flashed a crooked, semidrunken smile. The band suddenly clashed back into action, decibels louder than before. An invisible signal passed between the two men, and the talkative one yelled, "We want to talk to you."

"So talk. I'm all ears."

"Not here. Let's go in the back where it's quiet."

And deserted. "No thanks. I'm comfy here. Why don't you guys sit down?"

The mute grabbed my shoulders and lifted me from the stool. The effortless movement left me with a great deal of respect for his strength. I clutched my beer bottle and was propelled across the dance floor to a narrow corridor at the far end of the room. They pushed me into a small room and turned the lights on. The strong, silent guy leaned against the door.

Sweat trickled down my back. I looked around—
and laughed. "The bathroom! Jeez, you guys are real
cool. Is this your idea of a hot date?"

"Shut up. Why are you looking for Rudy?"

I slurred my words. "First you tell me to shut up,
then you ask me a question. Make up your mind." I
laughed and waved the bottle in the air; beer splashed
down my arm. I belched and covered my mouth. "Ex-
excuse me."

The guardian at the door spoke, "Man, she's shit-
faced. Come on, Mac. Let's get out of here before she
pukes all over your boots."

I giggled and swayed. "Hey, are you Rudy Mac-
Intyre? Man, I've been looking for you."

A fist pounded on the door. "Open up—I gotta
go."

MacIntyre shook a fist at me. "Listen, bitch, I don't
know you and I don't like strangers asking questions
about me. Stay the fuck away from me, or I'll let Duke
bash your face in."

The door shook as the fist pounded again. "Come
on, man. Open up—I really gotta go." MacIntyre and
friend stomped out. Another leather-clad man strode
in and immediately backed out, confused to find a
woman in his rest room. I splashed cold water on my
face and walked out, brushing past the man, who was
staring at the tips of his shoes. He looked confused. I
didn't stop to explain.

Rudy and Duke were gone. I sat at the bar and
smoked a cigarette, forcing myself to ignore the urge
to chase after them. The bartender smiled at me; I
mouthed an obscenity at him and headed outside to
find a cab. I found an empty street—not many taxis

cruise lower Manhattan at two o'clock in the morning. Hoping I'd find a cab on a busier street, I walked to Broadway.

There's a basic rule of survival in any big city: never walk too close to the buildings, especially at night. Someone could be lurking in a doorway or alley, waiting to pull you into the shadows. But I was tired and careless. I walked near the store fronts, thinking about bed, waiting for a cab to meander past. A gigantic hand darted out from between two buildings and yanked me into the darkness.

TEN

MUSCULAR ARMS WRAPPED around my rib cage, trapping my arms against my sides. I struggled and kicked. The arms tightened, squeezing the air from my lungs. I stopped fighting, afraid my assailant would crack a few ribs.

The powerful beam of a flashlight shone in my eyes. "Where's her purse? Find her ID."

This wasn't an ordinary mugging; I recognized the voice. I tried to turn my head away from the glare, but the light followed my movement. "MacIntyre—what the hell are you doing? Tell your gorilla to let me go. Promise I won't run away." Duke's arms contracted, and I decided to stop insulting him.

"Okay, bitch, you wanted to talk. Talk. Who are you, a cop?"

"I'm not a cop." But MacIntyre would never believe me. Then a car pulled up at the curb; the flashing red globe on its roof tinted our faces blood red.

"Shit. She is a cop!" MacIntyre dropped the flashlight and sprinted away. Duke had one last shot to deliver before following. He spun me around and smashed my face against the concrete wall. The sound of his boots hitting the pavement echoed in the alley.

Blood streamed from my nose. I sank to the ground, trying to remember if I should tilt my head up or down.

A car door slammed, and quick footsteps brought my rescuer to my side. He knelt beside me and put a hand on my shoulder. "Blaine, what's going down here? Are you okay?"

"Tony?" I lifted my head. He shined a flashlight on my face, pulled a handkerchief from his pocket and handed it to me. I pressed the cloth against my battered nose, said thanks, and asked, "What are you doing here?"

Instead of answering, Parker helped me to my feet and led me to his car, where he solicitously held the door and made sure I was safely inside before slamming it and running around to the driver's seat. When he opened his door, the overhead light went on. "Let me see your face. Shit, you're really bleeding. I'm going to take you to St. Kit's and have somebody take a look at you, make sure you're okay."

I gingerly touched my nose and winced. The cartilage was tender but in one piece. "Nothing's broken. The bleeding's almost stopped. I don't need a hospital. Just take me home."

"Okay." He slammed the door and sped away. Every time I asked Tony for an explanation of his timely arrival, he answered, "Let's get you home. We can talk after we get you patched up." I tried again, and Tony responded by saying, "You stink like you've been swimming in beer. Have you been drinking again?" I snapped that I hadn't; Tony pointedly rolled his window down. We didn't try to talk anymore.

As the car turned into Barrow Street, thoughts of Ida came to mind. I broke the silence. "Can you turn those overhead lights off? My nosy neighbors will be falling out their windows, trying to see who the cops are bringing home.''

Parker grunted and flipped a switch, killing the flashing lights. I relaxed. Ignoring the fire hydrant, he parked directly in front of my house and followed me up the stairs. Suddenly too exhausted to focus, I fumbled at the locks, unsuccessfully trying to get the door open. Tony watched without comment.

Fatigue overwhelmed curiosity. I wanted Parker to leave so I could go to bed. My questions would hold until morning. I finally managed to unlock the door and formed my mouth to spit out the correct words. "Thanks for coming to my rescue. I can manage from here. I'm going to take a few aspirin and go to bed.''

"Nope, you can't push me off like that. I'm coming in, I want to look at you under a good light. I just want to be sure you don't need stitches.''

My old sarge could be stubborn. We could stand on my front stairs and argue until I lost, or I could let him in. Giving in would be faster. I opened the door and walked back to the kitchen. Parker followed.

He pushed me to a chair and diagnosed my injuries as minor. Then he bustled around the kitchen, handing me a pack of ice cubes wrapped in a towel and making tea—for some reason, he decided coffee was the wrong beverage. I wanted him to leave, but a sip of tea revived my curiosity.

When Parker finally sat down, I found the energy to question him. "I'm not ungrateful, you got me out of a sticky situation, but I don't believe in happenstance. How did you just happen to be passing by that alley?''

He avoided my eyes. "Can't you say 'Thank you, Tony' and let it go?"

"No. You were a good teacher, I was a good student. I learned to keep asking questions until I get an answer. What were you doing there tonight?"

"I followed you."

My response was very mature for a person often accused of having a temper. I didn't scream or yell, I gently laid the ice pack on the table and looked at him. Tony's face was gray and drawn; the strain of command was making him a prematurely old man. I quietly asked, "Why were you following me?"

"I picked you up outside Blake's apartment. You should be more alert, young lady. You bounced a damn cigarette off the side of my car and didn't spot me. Things were quiet there so I decided to tail you."

Tony's nonchalant admission threw me off balance. I bypassed the obvious question of why he had really followed me, and went to a more important one. "Why were you staking out Hurley Blake's apartment? Hoping to see a ghost? Is bullying orphans and old ladies standard operating procedure for you?"

"Tony Parker is not doing anything wrong. I am involved in an ongoing criminal investigation and cannot discuss the details with you."

I drank some tea and smiled. The hot tea burned my throat and the smile made my face hurt. I put the ice pack against my face again and went to the sink for a glass of water. "I quit the force because I hated playing police games. Stop hassling the old lady. She's a pious Jesus freak who can't tell you anything except Bible quotes. Leave the kid alone too. All she knows is that her father's dead and the cops still won't leave him alone."

"Why are you so interested in their problems? You're not going to make any money from them."

His flippant comment enraged me. I tossed the makeshift ice pack into the sink and whirled around. "You don't understand, I'm trying to help the kid. Get the hell out of here. I want to go to bed."

Tony glared at me. I clenched my fists. He broke eye contact and rushed out; the door slammed. I unclenched my fists, plucked the towel from the sink and held it against my face to stem the trickle of blood dribbling from my nose.

BRIGHT SUNLIGHT on my face woke me. I didn't have to look at the clock to learn that, once again, I had overslept. I rolled out of bed and hurried to shower and dress. A puffy nose and brick burn on my left cheek were the only souvenirs of the previous evening. My attempts to cover my abrasion with makeup only made it more conspicuous. I washed the cosmetics off, resigned myself to a day of endless questions and went to make breakfast.

I was standing in front of the toaster, drinking coffee and watching a bagel slowly brown, when the telephone rang. Coffee mug in hand, I walked across the kitchen to answer it.

"Hello, Blaine." Don's quiet voice scared me. He heard my sharp intake of breath and said quickly, "Eileen's okay. She's awake. Can you stop by?"

"I think I can work a little visit into my busy schedule. I'm on my way." Even the smoke billowing from the toaster couldn't ruin the day. I pulled the plug, left the charred mess, and walked out of my house thinking it was time to find a cleaning lady.

Eileen had been moved from the intensive care unit to a private room on the fifth floor. The fifth floor was very exclusive territory, available only to celebrities and those willing to pay inflated prices for privacy. Extra security is a secondary benefit of the increased privacy: I wholeheartedly endorsed the move.

The security was good, but not good enough to stop a determined killer. While waiting for the special elevator I counted a half dozen ways to gain access to the VIP wing. Men and women in white lab jackets walked past the guards without challenge. Messengers pushing carts loaded with flowers nodded and walked past the security station. The staircases were unguarded and open to anyone wandering through. ID cards—easily duplicated or stolen—gave carte blanche to all who flashed them at the guard. Anyone carrying a chart was presumed to have the authority to pass. A priest hurried past the checkpoint without challenge. I stopped counting the ways past security and boarded the elevator.

Somber thoughts of Rudy MacIntyre accompanied me to the fifth floor, making me more nervous as each floor passed. The doors opened to a deserted lobby which led to an equally deserted corridor. My nerves jumped; hospitals are supposed to be busy twenty-four hours a day. Where were the people hurrying about on life-saving missions?

I walked faster. My soft-soled running shoes didn't make any sound. I crept down the empty hallway, wondering why I didn't see Brad's huge frame lurking in the corridor. The door to Eileen's room was closed. I slowly pushed it, pressed my ear to the slight crack, and listened. Eileen's weak voice was saying, "Don't—"

Happy that I'd chosen that morning to follow Brad's advice about taking precautions, I slid my pistol from its holster and darted into the room, ready for action. Brad, sitting on the wide windowsill next to the bed, stopped talking and laughed. "Here she is now, making quite a grand entrance." He glanced at the gun in my hand and raised his eyebrows. "Morning, Babe. Eileen was just telling me I shouldn't hang out here any longer."

"It's time for him to get back to work and start earning a salary again. I don't need baby-sitting." Eileen's voice was weak but adamant.

"You guys probably need to talk. I'll go make friends with the nurses; I haven't met the morning shift yet." Brad hopped off the ledge and started to walk past me, but stopped when he saw my face. He ran a gentle index finger down my bruised cheek and asked, "Hey, Babe, what happened to you? Your face looks like it went through a meat grinder."

I slid the automatic into my pocket and pointed to the door. "Go bother the nurses. I want to talk to my sister." Brad nodded and disappeared.

"What's wrong? What was Brad talking about?" The stiffness in Eileen's voice killed my urge to run to her side and hug her.

"Nothing happened. I just got a little scrape on my face. Brad exaggerates." I took Brad's place on the ledge and kept my voice level. "I found Rudy MacIntyre last night. Why didn't you tell me he came to the office?"

"He showed up one afternoon. I refused to see him. He left. There wasn't anything to tell."

Eileen's monotone frightened me. "Look what he's done. You have to talk about him. I want to nail this guy before he tries again."

"That's enough." A furious Dr. Mabe interrupted from the doorway. "I wouldn't let the police badger Eileen and I won't let you do it either. Try it again and I'll have you banned from this room. Eileen needs to get her strength back before you start throwing questions at her. Go wait outside, I want a few minutes alone with my patient."

Brad was lurking outside the room. He pointed at a chair and ordered me to sit. "You look beat, Babe. I'll get you a cup of what the nurses have the nerve to call coffee if you promise to tell me the truth about how you acquired that puffy nose and that equally gorgeous scrape across your cheek. I'd also like to know why you've become a pistol-packing mama again. Not that I'm complaining about the gun, Babe. I'm glad you finally took my advice—"

"I surrender!" I held up my hands. "Get the coffee. I'll tell you everything, just get the coffee."

Brad returned within minutes, carrying a black mug with a gold St. Kit's shield embossed on it. I took it from him, sipped the bitter brew, and asked, "Where's Don?"

"He left about half an hour ago to take the kid to the sitter. Then he's going to visit his office, or control tower, or wherever pilots go to arrange time off. He's going to need to spend time with Eileen. They'll be kicking her out of here soon—another week or so."

"Do you know everything that's going on in this hospital?"

He shrugged. "People like to talk to a big guy with a friendly smile. Everybody but you, Babe. As usual, you're trying to change the subject. I got the coffee, now I want the story. What happened?"

My brief recap of the previous evening was interrupted by Dr. Mabe. After another stern lecture, she allowed me to resume my visit with Eileen. Mindful of the doctor's warning, I let Eileen pretend she was recovering from minor surgery while I pretended I didn't notice the bandages over her eyes. We made polite conversation about her daughter, the office, and even the hot weather. I patiently waited for her to turn the discussion to more serious matters, but my patience wasn't rewarded. Eileen fell asleep without mentioning MacIntyre, the bombing, or her injuries. I gently kissed her forehead and left without giving Brad a chance to resume his many questions.

Since my day was ruined, I decided to spend the rest of it in the office, making case notes and catching up on paperwork. After a stop in the deli on the ground floor I took the elevator to my office and hoped my second attempt at breakfast would be successful.

The suite was quiet. A few people were wandering around organizing themselves after the awful week. I waved hello and ducked into my office before anyone could start a conversation that ended with questions about my bruised face and puffy nose.

I closed the door, pulled the lid off the container of coffee, unwrapped the bagel, and settled down for a peaceful brunch. After two swallows of coffee and a bite of the bagel, the telephone rang. Thinking it might be the hospital calling about Eileen, I grabbed the receiver. Jacob Faradeux's robust voice greeted me.

"Red, is that you? Son of a gun, you do work on Saturday. Nanci tried to make me wait till Monday. She said nobody in Manhattan works on Saturday. How the hell are you? I've got Nanci sitting here, glaring at me, so I got to behave myself. Clock's ticking, Red. We got a week till our party on Wall Street. I want to know how you're doing." There was noise in the background; Faradeux paused and came back on the line. "Hang on a second, Red. I'm gonna put you on the squawk box. Nanci keeps jabbing me in the ribs, asking me to tell her what you're saying."

I lit a cigarette and waited. The phone squealed, and Faradeux came back. "Red, you still there?"

"I'm here. Hi, Nanci. Is there anybody else with you?"

"Daddy and I are the only ones here. We took your advice. We're keeping our association with your firm top secret. We don't want to cause any more trouble for you, and we feel just awful about your sister. How is she?"

"Better." I didn't want to go into a long explanation. Jacob didn't give me a chance—he couldn't stay out of the conversation any longer.

"Glad to hear it. Your sister's a mighty fine woman. Okay, Red, tell me what you're doing for me."

"I'm making progress—"

"I don't see progress. I see another letter from those leaf-eaters in the mail, warning me off my business. What the hell are you doing to get them off my back?"

Nanci interrupted. "Daddy—"

I interrupted her. "Jacob, I'm not going to start a long-distance shouting match with you. I've infiltrated WARM's inner circle and will soon have access to their planning meetings. Be patient. Let me do my job."

Nanci quietly asked, "When are these planning meetings going to be held?"

I hesitated. Even though a meeting was scheduled for the following evening, I lied. "Sometime next week. They haven't set a definite date yet."

My lame answer satisfied the Faradeux clan. Jacob said, "Nanci and I will be in New York next week. We'll mosey over to your place to hear more 'bout your progress. See you next week, Red." He abruptly severed the connection without giving me time to answer.

So much for breakfast. I looked at the cold coffee and bagel with disgust. I swept the entire mess into the garbage and wondered why I found it necessary to lie to my clients. Intuition, obstinacy, or the fear their leak hadn't been plugged?

ELEVEN

JONA WALKED into my office holding a cup in front of her body like a shield. Convinced I was drinking too much coffee, she had recently developed the habit of bringing me decaffeinated tea in the afternoon. I always accepted the lifeless brew, thanked her, and waited until she left the room before dumping it into the plants on the credenza behind my desk. The plants loved the papaya mint tea and were flourishing under the decaf diet, so I never felt guilty.

"How late are you staying? You should be home taking it easy." The reproach in my secretary's voice was unmistakable.

"I'm leaving soon. You know, it's Saturday. Why are you here?"

She put the teacup on my desk and ignored my question, determined to issue a lecture along with the tea. "You've been working too much and you're not sleeping enough. You're smoking too many cigarettes and you're drinking too much coffee. You're going to wind up in the hospital with Eileen."

The tea smelled worse than usual. I looked at it and made a decision. I turned, poured the green stuff into the plants, and said, "Jona, you're right. I'm going home. I promise, I'll stop at a deli, pick up a nutritious dinner, take a long hot bath, and spend the evening reading. I also promise to go to bed early." And perhaps I'd stay there all evening, I silently added.

Approval brightened Jona's face. I closed the file I had been reading and followed her out of the office.

I MADE A QUICK STOP at a deli and then went home, intending to follow the promises I made to Jona. The annoying ring of the telephone greeted me when I opened the door to my house. I considered letting the machine answer but changed my mind and lurched for the receiver before the machine kicked in. My attempts to juggle briefcase, keys, mail, and groceries failed. I dropped everything. The seam of the thin plastic bag split, dumping oranges, cigarettes, and my salad bar dinner on the floor. The fruit rolled under the table, and a tiny pool of salad dressing formed under the broken container of lettuce.

My greeting wasn't cordial. I grabbed the receiver and snapped, "Hello. This better be important."

"Hello, dear. I hoped I'm not bothering you. This is Ida."

"No bother, I just got in." I smiled, knowing that she had an internal time clock, recording my comings and goings. Ida knew everything that happened on our block. "What's up? Do you need something from the store?"

"You're so sweet. No, dear, I don't need anything. My refrigerator is well stocked from the last time you went shopping. I'm calling because a package came for you today. I took it from your stairs so those ruffians who stand around on the corner wouldn't steal it. It's here on my kitchen table. Shall I bring it over?"

A warning shiver ran through my body; I wasn't expecting any packages. I tried to keep my voice calm. "Ida, don't touch it. Get out of your house, it could be dangerous.'' Ida tried to interrupt, and I shouted, "Leave it alone! Get away from it, get away!''

A low rumble shook the house. I dropped the phone and ran at top speed across the street, knowing it was too late.

Ida's front door was no match for my desperate strength. I kicked it open. Mikey's ghastly howls greeted me. Two steps into the kitchen I skidded to a halt, horrified by the sight. Bits of plaster, glass, crockery, and skin littered the floor. It was too late, much too late, to help Ida.

I forced myself to the mangled body, propelled by the illogical hope that it wasn't her. My feet slid on the floor, and I looked down. I was standing in a crimson pool of blood, its surface flecked with plaster and bits of brain tissue. I blindly ran outside and vomited all over Ida's neat flowerpots.

A COP FOUND ME sitting on the curb, shivering and staring at the blood on my sneakers. He waved a gold shield in front of my eyes. "You found her?"

I couldn't stop shaking long enough to answer. The cop snapped a capsule and waved it under my nose; the ammonia fumes brought tears to my eyes. Coughing, I pushed his hand away. The dry heaves struck, and I bent over and choked through the attack. The nameless cop put an arm around my shoulders and patiently waited until I caught my breath.

"The neighbors said you went running into the house shortly after the explosion. What happened?"

I choked again and fought to catch my breath. We sat on the curb and I told my story, ignored by the crowd of onlookers who were busy watching the cleanup crew scurry in and out of Ida's house. We moved across the street to my house, where I sat at the kitchen table and dazedly answered questions.

Men in ill-fitting suits drifted in until a half dozen were gathered in my kitchen. They methodically recorded everything I said in tiny notebooks and asked the same questions over and over again. Parker walked in and stood in the doorway. He listened, carefully watching my face while I spoke. I finished and looked at Parker. The lines in his face had deepened and multiplied since our last encounter.

"That's it?" I nodded. Parker wasn't satisfied. "Did she say anything about the package? What did it look like? Who left it?"

I shook my head helplessly. Annoyed by my muteness, Parker snapped. "What did the old lady tell you? Think."

"She said..." My voice cracked. I cleared my throat and tried again. "She said she took the package from my front steps so no one would steal it."

"What time was it delivered?"

"I don't know."

"Did she get a look at whoever left it?"

"I don't know."

"How big was it?"

"I don't know."

Tony angrily strode across the room and leaned over the table, his bloodshot eyes inches from my face. "Think, dammit! The old lady must have told you something useful."

"Ida said she took the package. She didn't say when it came or who left it. I heard the bomb explode and ran across the street.... I don't know anything else.

Did you look around her kitchen before you came over here?'' My voice rose. "Did you see what was left of her body before they scraped it off the floor? Don't tell me to think—I can't stop thinking."

"Hysterics won't help." Parker backed away. "Calm down. What have you been up to lately? Who'd want to send you a bomb?"

"We've been through this a dozen times. Find the guy who sent the bomb to Eileen and you'll find the guy who sent this one."

To my surprise, the answer satisfied him. Parker nodded and looked around the room, acknowledging the men gathered around. "Pack it up, guys. Let's call it a night." He hesitated as if he wanted to ask one last question, but changed his mind and turned to leave.

"Tony?" My questioning voice stopped him. "Can I have Mikey—Ida's parakeet? He's in her living room. There's no one else to take care of him."

Parker ordered one of the men to get the bird, then walked out without saying another word to me. The group of detectives evaporated as quickly and quietly as it had formed. I sat at the table, staring at my hands, unable to find the strength to move. A cop deposited the bird cage on the table, softly said goodnight, and left me alone with Mikey—and my guilt. I closed my eyes and saw Ida's body.

I opened my eyes and ran up to my bedroom to change into jeans. I also loaded my pistol and stuffed an extra ammunition clip into my pocket. I then grabbed my car keys and ran out of the house. I was going to find MacIntyre. When I found him, I was going to kill him.

MOST PEOPLE who live in Manhattan don't own cars. Those of us who do are often considered lunatics, slaves to alternate-side-of-the-street parking regulations, hardened to the sight of busted windows and stolen radios. But a car means freedom, the ability to flee the island without waiting for trains, buses, or rental cars—that's why we drag ourselves out of bed on cold winter mornings to search for a parking space on the other side of the street.

My car spends its leisure time safely locked away in a garage a few blocks from my house because I'm too lazy to get out of bed to search for a legal parking place. I retrieved the car and drove to Billy's Brewhouse, the only place I knew to find MacIntyre.

A Porsche, especially a bright red one, isn't the most inconspicuous vehicle to use for a stakeout, but I didn't have time to make other arrangements. I wanted Rudy MacIntyre. I parked a few doors away from Billy's and settled back to wait.

Two-seventeen. I was rationing my cigarettes and thinking about giving up when MacIntyre stumbled from the bar. He was alone. I smiled, stuffed a half-smoked cigarette into the ashtray, and slipped from the car. I followed MacIntyre down the empty street, my right hand confidently wrapped around the butt of the gun in my pocket and anxious for the opportunity to use it.

MacIntyre wobbled along while I walked behind, making no attempt to conceal my interest in him. He stumbled, and I sprinted to reach him before he regained his balance.

It's easy to overpower an unstable drunk—gravity is already trying to bring him down. One sharp jab in the back was enough to upend MacIntyre. He landed face down on the pavement and scrambled into an alley. I pushed him down and stuck my knee in his back. MacIntyre continued to struggle. I jammed the gun into the back of his neck, and he froze.

"My wallet's in my back pocket. Take it. Take whatever you want. Just be cool."

If I answered him, recognized him as a human being, I wouldn't be able to kill him. I pushed the gun deeper into his flesh.

MacIntyre stammered, "Come on, be cool. Take my money. Just be cool. Be cool."

I pushed the gun barrel into the hollow where his spine joined his skull. The hard steel of a pistol jammed into the nape of the neck sobers a drunk faster than gallons of coffee. MacIntyre stopped moving, stopped breathing.

"Tell me about the bombs."

"I don't know what you're talking about."

"Don't tell me you don't know. I'm just about ready to blow a hole through your fucking head."

"Shit, lady, be cool. I'm trying to be straight with you. But I don't know what you're talking about."

"Bombs, MacIntyre. I'm talking about bombs. The one you sent to my sister. The one you sent to Hurley Blake. The one you sent to my house."

"You gotta believe me, I don't know what you're talking about. I don't know you. I don't know your sister."

"You do know her. Eileen Aldridge, remember her? You tried to see her the other day. Then you tried to kill her. I think you're up to your old tricks and I'm going to stop you."

"I wanted to scare her. But Duke told me to lay off. Said she'd make trouble for me. Get my parole yanked. So I backed off. You gotta believe me. I don't know about any bombs." MacIntyre blubbered, "I'm telling you the truth, I only wanted to scare her. You gotta believe me."

I didn't believe him but I couldn't pull the trigger. I should have stayed in the car and shot him in the back as he walked down the street. I'm a good shot, I could have done it. Killed him without warning. The same way he killed Ida. The same way he tried to kill Eileen.

I took my knee away. MacIntyre rolled over and started to sit up. I held him down with the gun. "Don't. I'm still thinking about killing you."

TWELVE

INSTEAD OF KILLING MacIntyre, I went home. I slept for an hour or two, then spent the rest of the night in my rocking chair, staring at Ida's house. At dawn, I walked to the paper store on the corner to buy a few packs of cigarettes and every newspaper on the stand. Exhausted by the effort, I dragged myself home and collapsed on the sofa, the papers in my lap.

The bold headline on the top of the stack caught my eye. BOMB BLAST RIPS VILLAGE. A grainy photograph of EMS ambulances, police cars, and fire trucks haphazardly parked in front of Ida's brownstone filled the page. Telling myself it was a mistake to read the stories, I lit a cigarette and opened the paper.

A powerful bomb ripped through a quiet residential section of Greenwich Village early last evening, instantly killing the 77-year-old woman who had removed the package from the front stairs of a neighbor's house for safekeeping. Ida Yankovitch, a lifelong resident of the area, accidentally detonated the device when she attempted to return it. Police investigators declined to name the neighbor for whom the bomb was intended. They also refused to link the bomb to recent terrorist attacks.

Area residents expressed their shock and disbelief...

I dropped the paper. A sudden attack of blurry, tear-filled eyes made it impossible to read my neighbors' comments about Ida and their horror that such an incident could occur in our peaceful neighborhood.

The doorbell rang. When I stood up the *Daily News* slid to the floor. I stared at it. How long had I been sitting on the sofa, hypnotized by the picture on the front page?

The bell rang again. I stepped over the paper and yanked the door open. It was Dennis.

"I've been trying to call you."

"The phone's turned off. I don't feel like talking." When he didn't take the hint to leave, I asked, "What do you want?"

"I heard about last night's bombing. I want to talk to you about it." When I didn't answer, he walked inside and said, "Did you make coffee?"

"No. I don't have any. If you're desperate, there might be a jar of instant in the cabinet over the stove. Help yourself."

Dennis went to the kitchen, I went back to the sofa. He was gone long enough for me to smoke a cigarette. When Dennis walked into the living room, he was carrying two mugs. After handing me one of the cups, he sat next to me and tasted his brew.

I hate instant coffee. I put the mug down on the end table and lit another cigarette.

Dennis's eyes were drawn to the papers scattered on the floor. He nodded at them. "Licking your wounds?"

"That's not funny. Ida was..." Tears filled my eyes. I looked away from Dennis and nudged the papers with my toe. "It's my fault. After the attack on Eileen, I should have expected this."

"So what are you going to do about it, sit here and feel sorry for yourself? You haven't changed as much as you think. Why don't you just have a drink and forget everything?"

My face stung as if it had been slapped. "You bastard. Get out of here. Get out of my life." Tears rolled down my cheeks. I wiped them away, angry at Dennis, angry at myself for crying in front of him.

Dennis didn't move. I glared at him. "What do you want from me?"

"I came here because I'm worried about you. It's a damn shame your neighbor got killed, but snap out of this zombie routine before you get yourself killed. You can mourn Ida later, after we've caught this bastard." He paused for a second to be sure I was listening and then asked, "Who wants to kill you?"

I repeated my popular refrain. "Find the person who tried to kill Eileen and you'll find the person who killed Ida."

"You're wrong. The bombs were constructed by two very different people."

"Are you sure?"

"Positive. I saw the lab report before I came over here. They were able to give me a preliminary report. The components of your bomb were different from Eileen's. Yours was a claymore, filled with enough dynamite to blow anyone within twenty feet into tiny pieces. Your guy meant to blast you off the face of the earth." He waited for that information to sink in, then repeated his question. "Who wants to kill you?"

Dennis was destroying the neat theory I had developed during the endless night. All my suspicions shifted back to WARM, and I sighed. "I don't know, I don't keep a list of bad guys who hate me. No one's threatened me lately."

Dennis dismissed my answer with a wave of his hand. He rapidly fired questions at me, reaching back to half-forgotten cases of years ago. I finally protested, "Damn it, Dennis, you're very well informed about what I've been doing the past few years. Has the FBI been tapping my phones? Or have you been following me around, taking notes?"

"I've been interested."

Our eyes locked. I broke away and stood to look out the window, confused by the message I was receiving. "What do you want?"

"Cooperation."

"Personal or professional?"

"I want to review the cases you're working on as well as those you handled during the past three or four years. Hopefully, I'll be able to make some type of connection."

I shook my head and stared at the people walking along the street, wondering if my mad bomber was watching me. "I can't let you traipse through my files. That's confidential information. What do you think will happen when word gets out on the street that the FBI is rummaging through my files? I'll be out of business in minutes. Thanks for your concern, Dennis, but I'll pass—I can take care of myself."

"This is an official investigation. I'll get a search warrant."

"Go ahead. Try. You'll never get one. There's no probable cause. Nothing in my files was used for criminal activity. If you make an attempt to search my files, I'll get an injunction to stop you. Then I'll bring a civil suit against you and the FBI for violating my rights of privacy. You'll be sorry you ever tried to put your snoopy hands into my files."

"You are making a mistake. Whoever sent that bomb wants to kill you. He'll try again." I didn't answer. Dennis walked to the door and snapped, "Think about it. I hope you'll change your mind and cooperate." He stepped out, closing the door behind him with exaggerated care. I stared at it, wondering who won that round.

DESPITE BRAD'S heated advice to drop the Faradeux case, I went to the WARM meeting that evening, fully aware of the risk that my angry bomber might be there, waiting for me. At least the suspense would be over.

The regulars were gathered around the battered conference table, waiting for Roz to begin the meeting. I paused to scan their faces, watching for a guilty reaction. No one looked surprised to see me. No one, except Grant, looked happy to see me.

I slipped into the empty seat between Hodgkins and Grant. Hodgkins carefully studied my face, still trying to place me in his elusive memory. I turned to Grant, who grinned a sexy welcome and pressed a hot leg against mine. I ignored it.

Roz started the meeting. "Now that everyone's here, we can get started. As you know, Faradeux Industries is our next target. With a properly executed event, we will stop their ceremony and draw national attention to our cause."

Grant interrupted. "Roz, I'd like to say a few words. Leaks will not be tolerated. The police, the people at Faradeux Industries, and the Stock Exchange cannot learn of our plans. Breaches of confidentiality will be dealt with, immediately and harshly."

Was everyone staring at me? A furtive glance around the table revealed earnest faces watching Grant. He waited for a heartbeat to let the message sink in, then motioned for Roz to continue. She pulled an easel to the head of the table and unfurled a large map of the financial district. Pointer in hand, she indicated the building at the corner of Wall and Broad streets and began to lecture.

"Built in the early 1900s, the New York Stock Exchange is the symbolic center of the financial world. Many demonstrators have attempted to halt trading without much success. We have studied their attempts and learned from their mistakes. Our efforts will bring trading to a crashing halt. The entire world will condemn the immoral practices of Faradeux Industries and their unjustified oppression, exploitation, and killing of nonhumans so others might feast on their dead flesh. Specific assignments have been made—you will be contacted by your group leader and immediately begin work.

"There are five key committees. Technical Assistance will deal with flyers, posters, literature, telephones, copiers, walkie-talkies, fax machines, and other miscellaneous equipment. This operation will involve heavy expenses. We'll need bail money, lawyers' fees, supplies, and special equipment."

"What kind of special equipment?"

Roz's forehead wrinkled with annoyance at Hodgkins's quiet interruption. "We'll talk about that later." With the precise air of a military commander briefing her troops, Roz resumed her lecture. "The initial cost estimate is eight to ten thousand dollars. We have most of it but still need a few thousand dollars. We have plans to raise the money."

I didn't have to look at my tablemates to know they were staring at me. My assignment was obvious: write a check.

"Grant will talk about logistics."

Grant bowed mockingly. "Ladies and gentlemen, we are going to put on the biggest show the bulls and bears have ever seen. In just a few days, we are going to amass hundreds of people outside the Exchange. The workers who attempt to gain entry will be showered with red paint, symbolizing the blood of the innocent animals being slaughtered by the Faradeux greed machine."

His taunting smile chilled me. "If trading does start, we will stop it."

Roz quickly stood to wrap up. "We have a lot of work to do. Committees will begin work immediately." She folded her hands and stared at us. We were dismissed.

Roz, Collier, and Grant huddled in a private meeting while Amy and Hodgkins gathered up their books and briefcases. Amy left and Hodgkins started to follow her, then hesitated and walked over to me. "Would you like to join me for a cup of coffee?"

Grant overheard the invitation. Smiling above Roz's head, he mouthed, Wait for me.

Hodgkins's tan face tightened when I politely turned him down. My disappointed suitor whirled away and hurried after Amy, hoping for better luck. I lounged in my seat, trying to eavesdrop until Roz turned and frowned. Message received, I left the room.

Twenty minutes later, Grant stepped out of the elevator and looked around. I was sitting on top of the vacant security desk in the corner of the lobby, smoking a cigarette. Grant's somber face broke into a smile. "I'm glad you waited. Let's get out of here, I need a drink."

We walked to the end of the block and waited for the light to change. Traffic zoomed down Seventh Avenue. Grant impulsively wrapped his arms around me in a tight embrace, whispering, "I couldn't wait to see you again."

His hands moved up and down my back, caressing me. My paranoid mind jumped—was he searching for a gun? The light changed, and Grant slipped his arm around my shoulders and said, "Come on, let's go have a drink."

THIRTEEN

GRANT'S CHOICE for a quiet drink, a place called
A Big Country (SOMEBODY HAS TO DRINK IN IT! was
painted on the sign hanging over the entrance), was the
newest favorite watering hole in the city. Located on
Fifth Avenue, the bar was one colossal room. The
centerpiece was a room-length mahogany-and-brass
bar, raised on a pedestal. Five marble steps led to the
action.

The bar was packed with recent business and law
school graduates enjoying the New York City night-
life, courtesy of their expense accounts.

The hostess scanned us from head to toe and openly
sneered at our jeans. We weren't her typical patrons.
She passed us off to a waiter who led us to a tiny oval
table in a dark corner where the youngsters wouldn't
notice the two poorly dressed old-timers. Grant asked
for a wine list, quickly flipped through it, and ordered a bottle of Bordeaux. He looked at me and
bristled at my raised eyebrows. "What's the matter,
did I make a poor choice?"

I shook my head. "I wouldn't know—I don't drink.
This isn't what I expected."

"You think I hang out in dumps and drink Bud-
weiser from the bottle. Don't underestimate me. I like
pretty women and I don't like taking them to filthy,
smelly bars."

The waitress returned, the ritual of opening a bottle of wine interrupted Grant's outburst. She labored with the cork, eventually managing to wrestle it from the bottle in one piece. Grant impatiently waited for her to return with my seltzer, then lifted his glass and gently tapped it against mine. "To the success of Faradeux Day. And to us."

Sometimes a woman's best defense is silence. I smiled like the Mona Lisa.

Grant leaned closer, fixing his brilliant eyes on my face. "What did you think about the meeting? I'd like to hear your impression."

"It was interesting. Roz almost smiled at me."

"She's beginning to accept you. I told you she would loosen up."

"A few thousand dollars will buy a lot of acceptance."

Grant was smart enough to not act stupid. "You're upset."

"Of course I'm upset. What do you expect? It's obvious I'm being tolerated because of your inner circle's erroneous assumption that I'm a rich widow who can be sweet-talked into bankrolling your operation."

"Everyone has to contribute what they can. Some are called to contribute their time and talents. Others—"

"Bullshit. Would I have been invited to your meetings if you didn't think I had money?"

"I wanted you before the question of money came up. The others were hesitant about taking you in, and the possibility of your contribution silenced their doubts."

I flatly said, "I don't have the money."

Grant's mouth twitched. He got it under control and mumbled, "But you said..."

"I said I didn't have to work, I said I wasn't rich. You didn't listen."

A streak of anger flashed through Grant's beautiful eyes; an impenetrable shield quickly replaced it. "I'm listening now."

"It's difficult to explain, I sound so stupid." I fumbled with a cigarette, and Grant gallantly held a match to it. "My husband always handled our money. I never knew what was going on with our finances. I didn't care, I was busy with my photography—that's what I do, I'm a photographer. Jeff gave me money when I needed it, I'd give him the bills. It sounds stupid, but the arrangement worked." I took a deep drag of the cigarette. "Jeff set up a trust fund in his will so I wouldn't have to worry if something happened to him. My attorney administers it...."

"Can't you ask him to send you a check?"

I looked embarrassed. "I get an allowance. I'm already over my quarterly limit. My next payment is due in three weeks. If I try to get more money before then, my attorney will ask thousands of questions. Questions you don't want me to answer." I decided to leave some hope. "I have a little cash, but nothing close to what you need."

Grant couldn't hide his disappointment. He drained his glass and refilled it before answering. "Roz will be more sympathetic if you come up with something. How much can you get?"

Rapid calculations whirled inside my head. What would be a good number?

"A few hundred." Grant's face reflected his displeasure. I sighed. "I could probably scrape up five, six hundred. Maybe a thousand." Petty cash would scream. "It's just... Never mind." Avoiding Grant's eyes, I took another hit on the cigarette.

"What?" Grant rubbed the back of my hand. "What's wrong?"

"I'm being used. Not by you. You're on my side. It's the others. Once they know I can't give them a lot of money, they'll toss me out." I covered his hand with mine. "Grant, this means a lot to me. I want to be part of WARM. Let me help plan the big event."

Grant squeezed my hand. "This place is too crowded. Let's go someplace where we can be alone."

Tempting, but the old cliché about not mixing business and pleasure—especially deadly business— sounded. I turned him down; he wasn't crushed by my refusal. We made plans to meet again in a couple of days in a different bar. The meaning of Grant's invitation was clear. I'd better have money in my pocket.

ANOTHER MONDAY MORNING, another diasastrous beginning. Nanci Faradeux sat in the lobby, hands clenched in her lap, the ragged edges of her fingernails betraying a nervous nibbler. She caught sight of me and jumped to her feet, kicking over the briefcase at her feet.

I had decided to start the week off with an early visit to Eileen. Nanci's urgent request for a meeting caught up to me at the hospital. I hurried across town, grateful for the excuse to get away from Eileen, whose recuperation was marked by rounds of sarcasm, bouts of bitterness, and nonstop questions about minute business details. My inability to give satisfactory answers ignited Eileen's fury.

"Irritability and anger—that's what you should expect from Eileen. Grin and bear it until she finally confronts her fear and deals with it." Dr. Mabe's explanation for Eileen's behavior sounded reasonable, but following her advice was becoming more difficult every day. I left the hospital to meet Nanci, relieved and guilty for feeling relief.

Nanci's apologies began when we shook hands and continued during the short walk to my office. I sat her down, poured two cups of coffee, and passed one to her. "Please, stop. I was glad to get away from the hospital. What brings you to town? Is Jacob with you?"

"Daddy's still in Texas. He doesn't know I'm here." She put the coffee cup down, not trusting her shaking hands. "I didn't dare tell him I was coming to see you."

"You flew up here just to see me?" Nanci nodded. I shook my head and said, "People don't fly across the country just to have coffee with me. What's wrong?"

"It's my brother, Benji. Benji betrayed Daddy, betrayed the company. I don't know what to do, Daddy will kill him."

"What did Benji do?" Nanci didn't need more encouragement, and her story spilled out. I lit a cigarette and sat back, concentrating on understanding her Texas-tinged voice. "Being the oldest, Benji always assumed Daddy would pass the company reins to him. But Daddy didn't agree, he said Benji would ruin the company. Benji swore he'd destroy the company, he said no one would have anything. Benji can be sullen and hateful, but I never thought he'd actually try to destroy the company. Not until last night...."

Nanci was having trouble describing her brother's actions. I stubbed my cigarette out and quietly asked, "What's Benji done?"

She took a handful of papers from her briefcase and tossed it on the desk. "I found these. I didn't know what to do, that's why I decided to come here."

The papers confirmed my theory about an informant inside Faradeux Industries. The first, a facsimile sent to a 212 area code, which would probably match the number on the fax machine in WARM's office, contained the news that Faradeux had hired my firm "...to investigate legal methods of stopping the demonstration."

On the morning after the bombing, I acted on an impulse and called Jacob and Nanci to suggest a little scheme to take the pressure off. The second fax showed that my advice had worked. The message congratulated WARM "...for taking decisive action. The firm has withdrawn. There are no plans to engage another."

The third communiqué was terse. "Have read your plans. I encourage you to proceed. Through our actions, we will end the oppression of those species who are unable to protect themselves from our killing machines." I carefully placed the paper on top of the others and looked at Nanci. Ashamed to be carrying the news of her brother's betrayal, she avoided my eyes.

"Where did you get these?"

"Benji's drinking more than a parched cow in July. He said he had to work yesterday, to catch up on correspondence. When he didn't come home for dinner, I went into his office and found him dead drunk, passed out at his desk. The file was on the floor, papers scattered all over. I picked them up. After I read the first one, I ran to make copies. I was so afraid he'd wake up and notice. When I finished making copies, I threw the file on the floor and left. Benji hadn't moved, he never noticed. What should I do?"

I snapped my fingers against the copies and thought out loud. "Pretend you never saw these. Go back to Texas."

"What are you going to do?"

"Nothing." Nanci's face was blank. I tapped the papers again. "These don't prove anything, your brother doesn't say anything incriminating, they aren't even signed. Look, you took a hell of a chance by sneaking them from your brother's office, but I need solid proof. Go back home, keep your eyes open. Just don't do anything foolish. Whatever you do, don't tell anyone about them or your trip up here."

I never heard Nanci's response; the intercom sounded its obnoxious buzzer before she could speak. Jona's voice clearly reflected anxiety. "Blaine, there's a man on the phone. He won't give his name but he insisted on speaking with you. It sounds important. He said you met him last night."

"I'll take it." Nanci nodded her understanding. I grabbed the receiver and whirled around in my chair to face the window.

"Do you know who this is?"

"Yes, I do. What do you want?"

"I've been rapping out with the homeboys. I'm a stand-up guy, so people talk. You'll be wanting to hear from me."

"Talk. I'm listening."

He laughed obscenely. "Lady, I got expenses. Talk don't come cheap."

"How much?"

"Five bills."

It was my turn to laugh. "You have a very high opinion of yourself. Tell me your story, then I'll decide how much it's worth."

MacIntyre thought for about fifteen seconds. "You know that little lake in Central Park? The one where the kids sail their little boats? Be there in half an hour. Bring some cash 'cause you're gonna love my story."

MACINTYRE'S CALL didn't leave me any time for advance planning. In the midtown lunch rush, it's difficult to move from Fifty-fourth Street to Central Park in less than half an hour, no matter which method of transportation you use. I left Nanci sitting in my office and hurried from the building, unsettled about not being able to check the site out in advance.

Walking would be just as fast as the subway or a cab. I crossed Central Park South, dodging taxis and hansom cabs, and entered the park, heading for the little lake near Seventy-second Street that's called the Conservatory Pond in most guidebooks. Some prehistoric funding crisis killed the project before the greenhouse could be constructed but the pond survived, delighting the kids—young and old—who use it to sail their remote-controlled yachts.

I stopped at the top of one of the twin staircases leading down to the pond and scanned the area, trying to spot MacIntyre or his pal. The sidewalks and benches around the water were crowded with schoolchildren on recess and workers from the nearby hospital and offices luxuriating in the warm sunshine.

No sign of MacIntyre. I ran down the stairs, purchased a hot dog from the brick concession stand, and found an empty bench. After one bite of the hot dog, I jumped up to prowl around, checking out all the places where Rudy and friend could be hiding with a pistol, waiting to take me out of the investigation. There were too many secluded hiding places. My appetite disappeared. I tossed the half-eaten hot dog into a trash can and lit a cigarette.

MacIntyre appeared during my second lap around the tarn. He swaggered down the path at the northern end of the conservatory area and fell into step beside me as I rounded the top of the oval. The lunch crowd was making its way back to work, leaving behind empty benches and overflowing garbage cans. We sat on a bench next to the refreshment stand and stared at each other. MacIntyre's eyes were crusty and bloodshot; he blinked and hastily slammed his sunglasses on.

"Did you bring your money?"

"Did you bring your story?"

"Maybe. If the pay's good enough, I'll talk."

I pulled a brand-new crisp fifty-dollar bill from my pocket and handed it to him. It crackled when he grabbed it. "Here's a down payment. Now talk. There's more, if I like what I hear."

"I got curious about this Blake dude, so I asked around. He was no choirboy. Blake may have told you he was straight but he wasn't. He started running numbers and worked his way up to bookie—"

"Ancient history. Tell me something I don't know."

"The brother was back in the business. 'Cept he was high class, wouldn't deal with scum off the street." MacIntyre leaned closer. "He had select clientele, if you know what I mean."

I moved away from his stale breath and said, "I don't know what you mean. Spell it out."

The silence was broken by the crackling sound of another crisp fifty hitting MacIntyre's palm. His power of speech quickly returned. "He didn't want to be hassled by the cops so he became bookie to the pigs."

"Parker's a cop. He hassled Blake a lot."

MacIntyre's coarse laughter stopped me. "Lady, he had a real big marker with the brother. An old one, but a very, very big one. It was on hold but Blake was getting greedy. Parker wanted to put the brother out of business before it got called. Every time he tried, Blake's sharp mouthpiece got him off."

At least Eileen had been doing good work. It's too bad she didn't know the truth about Hurley Blake's business—she could have charged instead of letting it go as pro bono work. I shook my head. "Are you sure about this marker? How reliable is your information?"

"Got it from a righteous brother. He told me—" Suddenly realizing he was about to give away information without charging, Rudy stopped. "My homeboy don't come cheap. Fifty bucks ain't gonna make him talk."

"You'll see more cash after I hear more. Tell me about this marker."

MacIntyre shrugged. "There ain't much to tell. My homeboy hangs with the old dudes; they told him 'bout it. The marker's so old, it's ancient. Gotta be five, six years old."

I slid two more bills into MacIntyre's hand. "Talk to your homeboy again. Find out about the marker. Call me when you know more about this marker. Call me with real information and I'll double this." I stood.

"Hey, lady, chill out and sit tight. I ain't done. Blake was into some real heavy shit. Lots of people are gonna be missing Mr. Hurley Blake. 'Specially those who wanted his 'Nam connections."

Our little section of the park was empty; lunchtime had come and gone. The bright sunlight made the desolate spot more sinister. I shivered and snapped, "Get on with it, MacIntyre. I can't spend all afternoon sitting on a park bench, listening to your bullshit. I'm not paying you by the hour, give me something real."

MacIntyre grinned. "Be all you can be. The olive drab brothers at Dix been lifting shit from the ammo closet. Blake was their main swing man."

My brain churned out an English translation while Rudy spoke. "Was Hurley Blake fencing stolen arms?"

MacIntyre nodded impatiently. It wouldn't be long before he popped off the bench searching for another fix. I hurried another question. "Was Blake dealing anything beside guns?"

"Oh yeah. He could get anything, anything at all. Anything the army can buy with your tax money. Leave an order with the shopkeeper, leave enough bread. Get whatever you want. Machine guns, rifles, missiles, bombs."

MacIntyre's smug smile annoyed me. I wanted him out of my sight. I stripped another bill from my cache and dangled it over his greedy palm. "Find out about that marker." I'm never sure how to note payments to informants on my expense report, but I decided to go for it. I dropped the money into MacIntyre's hand. "Like I said, the rate's doubled if you come up with something solid."

MacIntyre stuffed the bills into his shirt pocket to join the others. "Yeah, yeah. I hear you. I'll call you. Tell your prissy secretary she shouldn't leave me hanging on hold—I might get pissed and hang up." He tipped an imaginary hat and strutted away.

I smoked a cigarette and watched the nannies and the afternoon sailors launching their boats. Everything looked so normal, so perfect. I yawned, crushed the cigarette underfoot, and slowly walked back to the office, digesting MacIntyre's information as I walked.

FOURTEEN

EILEEN NEVER MISSES an opportunity to tell me to finish my law degree. I always laugh and say I don't want to be running in and out of court like she does, lugging twenty pounds of papers under my arm. I looked at the papers spread across my desk and rubbed my aching temples, wondering if it was too late to follow her advice.

I was stuck. Like a cartoon painter, I'd investigated myself into a corner and couldn't get out. Endless cups of coffee and a pack of cigarettes didn't shake any ideas loose from the back of my brain where they had stubbornly lodged. I decided to get out. I walked across town to St. Katherine's, hoping Eileen had a good day, hoping she would be willing to listen to my problems.

Eileen didn't want to hear my problems but I heard plenty about hers. After half an hour of listening I escaped from her clutches and ran out of the hospital. I stopped at the curb, gratefully inhaled the warm sweet spring air, and walked home. Thoughts of the dark house and the ruins of Ida's house pushed me off course. I headed for the View.

THE BAR WAS PACKED. I slumped in the doorway, dejectedly searching for an empty stool, spirits crashing. Ryan noticed my lost orphan look, winked sympathetically, and filled a mug with seltzer. He swung the mug across the bar, saying, "Hang in, sweetie, the tunnel rats will be rushing for their buses soon. This one's on me, just don't tell Bobby—he'll yell."

I grabbed the soda and, without spilling a drop, pushed through the crowd to the cigarette machine. I leaned against it, waiting for an empty seat, when a familiar face approached. The man was too intent on the mission of acquiring tobacco to notice me.

"Jose." I touched his arm. He looked at me and grinned. It was a nice change to have a cop smile at me—lately they'd been frowning every time I came near. "When did the View turn into a cop bar?"

He laughed. "It's not. Carmelita's fed up with cops, cop bars, and cop talk. She threatened to leave me if I took her to a place that was filled with cops. After fifteen years, I listen to her threats. That's why we're here—no cops. How's your sister?" He dumped a load of quarters into the machine and made a selection; a pack of Marlboros dropped out. "Come sit with us. Carmelita will love to see you."

We wove through the crowd to a booth near the kitchen and to Carmelita, Jose's dark-haired wife. She tried to spot her husband in the crowd and saw me trailing behind; the welcoming smile made her plain face beautiful.

With the quiet resignation of a cop's wife, she said, "I am sure you want to talk about the Job," giving it the capital J all cops' spouses use.

I was ruining her evening, but I nodded and asked Jose, "What's with your boss? He's been looking pretty grim lately."

Jose was not oblivious to Carmelita's unhappiness. He tasted his beer and said, "Parker? He's okay, lots of pressure, but he's okay."

"The man loves pressure. He's bored when things are quiet. There must be some pretty heavy stuff going down—he looks like hell."

Jose peered at me over the top of the beer mug. "There's rumors."

I waited. Carmelita sighed. Jose patted her hand, asked for patience, and continued. "The gossips are saying Parker's lobbying for a new assignment. He's in the running for some new task force on juvenile offenders the mayor's putting together. Mulchakey was the number one man for the spot but a skeleton fell out of his closet and put him out. Skeletons in the closet—they'll get you every time."

Carmelita's long impatient fingers started spinning the pretzel dish. I glanced at her and quickly looked back at Jose. "I haven't heard anything about this task force. What's so special about it?"

"Publicity. Self-promotion. Everything a climber needs to climb. Parker wants out of the scum-filled Forty-ninth, thinks he'll do better trying to keep the kids in line. At least he'll be in the papers every day. His face will be all over the evening news, talking about what he's doing to get the kids to put down their forty-fives and to stop killing each other for their coats. Next stop, police commissioner—or so he thinks."

Carmelita stirred and vocalized her distaste for our conversation; I had run out of time. We spent the rest of the evening talking and laughing about the Mets, the Yankees, tuition bills, and the unpredictable behavior of thirteen-year-old girls.

SKELETONS IN THE CLOSET. I went to bed at three, thinking about the way Jose smiled when he said "Skeletons in the closet." I slid into that nebulous state preceding sleep where dreams mingle with reality, when Jeff's voice whispered to me.

The skeletons were in the attic—not the closet. I snapped awake and scrambled out of bed, pillows and blankets tumbled to the floor.

I dressed in clothes suitable for rummaging in a dusty attic and ran up the stairs. The naked bulb hanging from the center beam wasn't very strong, but it threw off enough light for me. Even in total darkness, I would have been able to find the chest sitting in an isolated corner, carefully separated from the rest of the junk. I approached it with trepidation.

The trunk was filled with objects too precious to throw away, too painful to keep in sight. Five years ago, I had rushed through the house, gathering everything that reminded me of Jeff, threw it all into that oak box, slammed it shut, and dragged it across the rough wooden floor, sobbing as I pushed and pulled and kicked it to its final resting place under the attic window. With shaking hands, I reached out to loosen the tarnished brass hasps, took a deep breath, and swung the lid open.

Relics from Jeff's career as a drug enforcement agent greeted me. Even through the distance of time, the pain was immediate and real. Tears blurred my eyes; I impatiently rubbed them and began searching.

What was I looking for? I didn't know—a dream had sent me to the attic, the dream would have to guide me. I burrowed through files, pictures, books, and other memorabilia until my fingers touched Jeff's notebooks. I pulled them free and stacked them next to the trunk. After adding a dozen manila files to the pile, I had enough. Leaving the trunk open, I carried my treasures downstairs to spread them out under the bright kitchen light.

Jeff had precisely recorded names, dates, and other details of his cases—had stored them for the novel he always threatened to write. The last entry in his notebook described plans for the botched drug raid that killed him. I stared at the list of cooperating agencies and the contacts from each, picking familiar names from the list, touching each with my index finger, feeling the tears gather. Parker, Halstead, O'Brien, Ferguson, and others—it was amazing how many of these people still wandered through my life. I closed the book. I knew how the story ended. Plans for the raid had been leaked, and Jeff and two other agents were killed. The skeletons, if they existed, remained well hidden.

Six o'clock. It was too late to sleep and too early to do anything else. The house could use a cleaning but I wasn't desperate enough to plunge into mopping and dusting. I took a shower, and thought about going to the office. That bad idea disappeared down the drain, replaced by thoughts of swimming. I found my bathing suit hanging in the bathroom where I'd left it after my last swim, and slowly wandered through the sleepy streets to the Y on Eighth Street. Stuck between a topless bar and a used-book store, it wasn't in the best neighborhood, but at six in the morning no one would be out on the street, and the pool's lanes would be empty.

I changed, threw my clothes into a locker, and padded out to the pool. A solitary swimmer was in the center lane, making the turn at the near end of the pool. Diving in just as she finished her turn, I matched her stroke for stroke. We made the far turn at the same time and headed back. The competition was even until midway across the pool, when she sprinted and pulled away, touching the tiles two strokes ahead of me.

The woman pulled herself up on the side of the pool and turned to me, a satisfied smile on her face. I gasped, "Nice kick. I couldn't keep up. I was eating cold pizza at four-thirty this morning, guess it slowed me down."

"Honey, you are always making excuses. Give it up, I'm faster. Always was, always will be."

"Irma, you're a pro. I should have demanded three lengths' head start."

Three lengths wouldn't have given me much of an advantage. Irma wasn't a pro, but she would have been a starter on a U.S. Olympic team, probably a medal winner, if young black girls growing up in the South Bronx during the early sixties had had access to pools, trainers, and athletic scholarships. Defying family, friends, and stereotypes, Irma struggled into college, where a coach discovered her aquatic talents.

"I haven't seen you for weeks. Are you on your way to work, or home?"

"Home." Irma sighed and wiped a trickle of water from her face. "It was a long night. Couple of knifings, a rape, a murder, two attempted. All that blood left a huge pile of paperwork. And you know Parker, those reports got to be done 'on a timely basis.' Well, my basis sat at that damn desk until five o'clock. I've been pulling the overnight hours. You'd see more of me if you'd drag your lazy butt down here early enough."

"Stop insulting my lazy butt. Let's go have breakfast. My treat, I owe you."

Irma's a detective in the 49th Precinct. My breakfast offer was partially motivated by a long-standing tradition of the loser pays and partially by the hope I could do a little snooping.

I started to hoist myself from the water, but Irma pushed me back. "You are getting soft, two laps and you're ready to quit. I'm gonna do twenty more—I want to be hungry for that breakfast you're going to buy." She stood and bent to dive into the pool. "Try to stay close. It's embarrassing when you get so far behind."

Ten laps later, I was regretting the impulsive action that had dragged me to the Y. Pride got me through the remaining ten laps. Irma lapped me twice and sat on the edge of the pool, encouraging me to keep lifting my arms. I finished, rested my head against the side of the pool, and groaned.

"Girl, all the moaning in the world won't get you out of buying me breakfast. Now drag your lazy self out of that pool and get dressed. I'm hungry."

IRMA WAS A REGULAR in the coffee shop near the Y. The waitress set coffee down and asked, "The usual?"

"Two usuals. My friend's hungry too."

Irma weighs about one hundred pounds and has an appetite that would make a hungry lumberjack belch and surrender. I stopped the waitress. "Wait a second, what's the usual?"

She reeled off a list of food. I ordered fruit and toast and looked at Irma. "How do you manage to eat all that stuff and still fit into your bathing suit?"

"Metabolism. Got to have the right metabolism." Irma dumped three packs of sugar into her coffee and stopped laughing.

"So, lady, you're buying. What do you want to know?"

"You cops are so suspicious. Why do you think I want something? I offered to pick up the check so I wouldn't have to listen to you run your mouth about me being a welsher."

"You gave in too fast. I'm always suspicious when you don't argue about the bill."

I threw my hands up and laughed. "I'm a soft touch. But since you asked..." The waitress returned with plates of food, and I waited until she left before saying, "The thought did cross my mind that you could fill me in on some of the gossip." Irma's bushy eyebrows lifted and settled back. She poured syrup over the stack of pancakes on her plate and attacked them with a knife and fork.

"Parker was hassling a client, an East Village bookie. My informant tells me Parker had a sizable debt with the same bookie."

"He's always betting on things." Irma speared a sausage and thoughtfully chewed it. "Is this important? I can listen around."

"Parker expended a lot of energy trying to convince me to find a new client. My client died suddenly."

Irma dropped her fork. "I'm not going to help you hang a cop. Get yourself another girl."

"I'm not trying to hang Parker. He's been acting concerned one minute, threatening the next. I'm trying to figure out where he's coming from."

"Your eyes say something else. Be straight with me or I can't help you."

"When I was on the force, Parker was my rabbi. I don't want him to take the rap for anything unless he deserves it. Somebody tried to kill my sister—I'm chasing every lead, no matter where it takes me."

"If you don't do for your family, you're scum. Parker's my family." She sighed; I was ruining her appetite. "He's never made life any easier for me. He only helps a few, he don't like the rest of us. Like I said, I'll listen around. No promises." She yawned. "I gotta get some sleep. You better put in more pool time, you usually put up a better fight."

FIFTEEN

I WAS SPENDING too much time in bars, which is tough if you're an alcoholic. In a few short weeks, I'd been to uptown bars, downtown bars, terrorist bars, ex-con bars, leather bars, cop bars. I was on a first-name basis with every bartender in Manhattan, and finding it harder and harder to beat the urge to drink.

Grant's latest choice was a place called Lloyd's, lower Manhattan's version of an English pub. Lloyd's was filled with red leather chairs, heavy oak tables with tiny red candles in the center, and the accents of British expatriates. Grant rose from a table in a dim corner, waved, and hurried to my side. He kissed my forehead and said, "The guys in here don't give a beautiful woman much time alone."

"Am I supposed to blush and say 'Thank you, kind sir?' I don't know the rules of this game."

"I'm not playing—I'm serious. Let's not argue about a compliment." He took my arm and escorted me to our table.

I touched Grant's arm. "Sorry. I'm still a little touchy about this money business. I wasted half the night trying to balance my checkbook—it's a disaster area. There's no way I can come up with enough money to fund the rally."

"You have other talents. We'll find a use for them."

I wanted Grant to define which talents he wanted to use, but didn't ask. Anger bubbled below the surface of his face; my question would have caused an eruption.

"Lighten up, Grant, I came with good news. You're right, we have to contribute what we can, even if it means sacrifice. I can put a few bills off until the next quarter." I fumbled in my purse for an envelope and yanked it free, dropped it on the table between us. "It's all I can afford."

Grant's good manners kept him from snatching the envelope, and he motioned for a waitress and ordered two vodka martinis. I stopped the waitress and changed my order to seltzer. Grant casually picked up the envelope and slid it into his breast pocket. I asked, "Aren't you going to count it?"

"No, not here. How much is there?"

"Seven hundred and fifty." I waited for his reaction. The amount was a problem I had agonized over for hours. Too much would give Faradeux fits when I billed him for expenses. Too little wouldn't get me anything.

The volcano calmed down. Grant smiled and moved his shoulders so the envelope crinkled. "That's great. Roz is going to meet us here in a little while. She'll be pleased."

Was he nuts? Roz would never be satisfied. I swallowed a mouthful of the icy mineral water and shivered as it slid down my throat. Grant reassuringly patted my knee. "Don't worry. Everything will be fine."

As predicted, Roz blew in and scanned the room. Grant's head was bent too close to mine to notice her entrance. She frowned, and I nudged Grant to warn him but it was too late. She saw that he was paying too much attention to me. The frown deepened. Rosalynn settled into the chair next to me, acknowledging my presence with a cool nod. I reciprocated and lit a cigarette.

Grant's smile at the waitress produced another round of drinks. Roz swallowed half of her martini in one gulp, closed her eyes, then leaned back in the chair. I discreetly pushed Roz's glass farther away from me. I used to love martinis, and I wasn't in the mood to have a tempting, very drinkable martini so close to my hands.

"I hope your day was better than mine. It's been awful. I tried to find a new supplier, without much luck. I don't know what we're going to do—"

Smoke from my cigarette drifted past Roz's nose, reminding her that I was sitting across the table. She opened her eyes and drained the martini in one gulp, giving me a hostile look through the bottom of the glass. Grant nodded; a replacement magically appeared before Roz. Raising an eyebrow with the unasked question, Roz looked at Grant and tasted the drink.

Grant's happy voice rang through the quiet barroom. "I have great news. Blaine is going to help us." He patted his breast envelope.

"How much? Our costs have escalated because we had to find new suppliers. You won't believe how much money I had to pay out today."

"Slow down, honey. We'll get what we need. Blaine just gave me almost eight hundred dollars."

Roz's face reflected disappointment. She controlled her dismay and tried to smile, but a grimace crossed her face. "Eight hundred. Well."

Grant sat back, keenly interested in my reaction. I took a drag on my cigarette, searching for a delicate response that would hold the promise of more while giving me an idea of how they were going to spend my money.

A familiar voice called my name, and my stomach sank. Manhattan isn't very big. It's a tiny island made up of little villages a few blocks in length. People tend to stay in their little villages, and I had unwittingly wandered into Dennis Halstead's village. I sprang from the chair, quickly turning him away.

"Blaine, what a nice surprise! I didn't expect to see you here. Aren't you going to introduce me to your friends?"

"No—get out of here."

"What?" Puzzlement, then anger clouded his face.

I pushed him away from the table and whispered, "You idiot, did you turn your brain off when you left your office? I'm working. Please get out of here before I have to do a lot of awkward explaining."

Dennis glanced over my shoulder, then back at me. "Too late. That woman is staring. She's very interested in us."

"Shit. I can't blow my story this late in the case. You've got to help me. Can you play the old boyfriend role?"

Dennis laughed. "I've been playing that role for the past few days. It shouldn't be hard to convince your friends."

"Good. Do it, then get out of here before you blow my cover." Raising my voice loud enough for Roz and Grant to hear, I said, "I'm not going to tell you again. I don't want to see you."

I walked back to the table. Dennis followed. "And I'm getting tired of leaving messages on your answering machine. Why don't you return my calls?"

"I don't have anything to say to you. Leave me alone."

Dennis was enjoying his act. He grabbed my arm and painfully squeezed it. He gestured at Grant. "Who's that, your new boyfriend? Is he why you won't see me anymore?"

"I won't see you because you're a drunk."

"You—"

I raised my hand to slap his face. Dennis caught it and grinned. "Sorry, honey. I didn't mean to upset you. I'll see you around." He started to walk out of the bar, but changed his mind and sat at the bar.

I watched Dennis order a drink and shrugged; I'd scream at him later. When I turned back to the table, Grant looked concerned. "That guy's a troublemaker. Do you want me to ask the bartender to throw him out?"

"No. He'll go away if I ignore him. Sorry about the interruption." I looked at Roz. "Where were we?"

Roz ignored my question. She leaned across the table and asked, "Who is he, an old boyfriend?"

I groaned. "That's an old mistake. We dated a few times. Now he won't go away."

The cigarette I'd been smoking before Dennis's interruption was smoldering in the ashtray. I stamped it out and took another cigarette from the pack. Grant snatched the matchbook from my hands and lit the cigarette.

"Can we get back to business?" I asked.

Grant kicked Roz under the table, and she started talking. "We've been guilty of underestimating you. Taking in a new person is always a slow, painful process. There've been so many betrayals...."

Roz's half-assed apology parched her throat; she snatched her glass from the table and swallowed the martini. I smiled, cheered by the thought that Roz was going to have a wicked hangover in the morning.

Grant jumped into the void. "We have an important mission for you. The cops know us, but they don't know you. They aren't watching you. We want you to stop attending the meetings in our office, in case we're under surveillance—"

"You got money out of me, but it isn't enough, so you're going to cut me out of the action. You lying bastards."

"You're wrong," Roz insisted. "We're offering you a larger role in the organization. The police don't know you—we're going to use that. It's your greatest strength. After tonight, Grant is the only member of the organization you'll have contact with. He'll keep you informed."

"What's this new important role? I've already played banker. What's next, Roz, postman?"

"We need a safe house. A place to store our supplies. Things we can't leave in the office."

"Drugs, money, guns, or explosives? What are you trying to hide?"

"That's on a need-to-know basis only. We'll tell you in due time."

"Roz, it's my basement you're proposing to use as a hiding place for your toys. My butt winds up in jail if there's a bust, not yours. I need to know. Now. Before anything moves into my house.''

Her eyes rolled to Grant. His hand moved under the table and came to rest on my leg. "Don't worry. We're not asking you to do anything dangerous. Think about it. We'll get together tomorrow.'' Grant named a different bar as our next meeting place and they walked out, leaving me to settle the bill.

Dennis watched them leave, then sauntered over. He plopped into a chair without waiting for an invitation—he'd still be standing if he'd waited. "Your friends left in a hurry. Is your business done?''

I glared at him. "What are you trying to do, put me out of business completely? Why didn't you get out of here?''

"I decided to hang around in case you needed backup.''

"Who appointed you my protector? I can take care of myself. When I need backup, I'll ask for it. Brad's quite good at it.''

He opened his mouth and closed it, swallowing an angry rejoinder. "Did you have dinner? I have two steaks in the refrigerator. We can buy some stuff for a salad. I'll cook.''

"How can you do that? How can you change the subject like nothing happened?''

"I'm trying to apologize but you won't let me. I'm sorry. I'm sorry. I'm sorry. How many times do you want me to say it? I'm sorry. I'm sorry.''

"Shut up.''

"I'm sorry. I'm not going to stop until you forgive me. I'm sorry.''

"Dennis—don't push me. It's been a lousy day, my case is going into the sewer, and you're having a good time busting my ass. Leave me alone."

He stopped laughing. "I am sorry. I thought I was being helpful but I was just overreacting."

"You were being stupid."

"I was being stupid. Is that enough? Let's have dinner, a friendly dinner. No fighting, I promise."

His brown eyes were sincere. He was a good cook. My refrigerator was empty. I was hungry and tired of arguing with people. I accepted. What else could I do?

DENNIS'S APARTMENT was on the tenth floor of a rent-controlled oasis in the midst of thousands-of-dollars-a-month luxury towers. The security guard ignored us as we walked past his little desk in the lobby. He ignores everyone, preferring to pass his shift with his eyes steadily fixed on the small television under the counter. Canned laughter trailed after us to the elevator.

I followed Dennis to the living room and whistled softly. "You found a cleaning lady."

Dennis, whose housekeeping skills consist of an amazing ability to ignore dirt and chaos, laughed. "It got to the point where even I couldn't stand the mess. And you're being sexist. I didn't find a cleaning lady—I found a cleaning man."

Dennis anticipated my question and quickly interrupted me. "Don't ask, I won't give you his name. Find your own cleaning man." He carefully draped his suit jacket over a chair, loosened his tie, and rolled his sleeves up over his elbows. "You can watch me cook if you promise to stay out of the way."

The cramped kitchen was barely large enough for two adults. I perched on a stool and watched Dennis work. By mutual consent, all work-related talk was banned. Our conversation briefly touched on the dissolving marriages of old friends, then quickly drifted to restaurants, museums, theaters, and other things that make city living bearable.

We set trays up in the living room and ate in front of the television, watching the Mets blow a game, hoping a sudden monsoon would save them. During the seventh-inning stretch, the announcers recapped the lack of action, repeating the sad lament of the season: "Once again, the Mets' hitters are unable to support the fine performance of the pitching staff...." Dennis hit the mute button. I glanced at him and quickly looked away, confused by the sudden rush of affection that hit.

I struggled from the grasp of the soft cushions and fled to the kitchen with the dinner plates. Dennis came in while I was watching the sink fill with water. He tried to squeeze behind me to place the glasses he was carrying in the sink, an impossible maneuver in the diminutive kitchen. His arms went around my waist, dropped the glasses in the soapy water, then wrapped around me.

From the instant I had accepted his dinner invitation, we both had known how the evening would end. I leaned back against him and said, "I miss you."

"I miss you, too."

I peeled the rubber gloves from my hands, tossed them in the sink, and turned to Dennis. We left the dishes for his anonymous cleaning man.

I remembered every line, every curve of his body. Guided by memory, we came together in a passionate burst of energy that left us drained and breathless. Breaking the silence that settled over us, I turned to Dennis and whispered, "Are you asleep?"

"No." He took my hand and gently stroked my knuckles. "I was watching you."

"Can I trust you?"

"You just did." He kissed my fingers. "I may be arrogant, obnoxious, and insensitive, but I'm always trustworthy. What do you want?"

"Something's bothering me. I need to talk."

"Is it us that's bothering you? Because if it is, don't worry, things will be different this time. You can trust me."

This time? I bit down on my tongue; I didn't remember making any commitments. "That's not the problem. What do you know about nails?"

"Nails? I don't understand— Oh, yes I do...." Dennis dropped my hand and pushed himself to a sitting position. His voice was expressionless. "You want to talk about work. I was hoping you wanted to talk about us."

"Don't be angry. I need to talk to someone I trust." I crossed the chasm that had opened between us and rubbed my hand along his thigh.

He brushed my hand away. "Not during work."

"Dennis, please..."

Seconds away from battle, we stopped talking. Pulling away from him, I rolled on my side and stared at the wall. I took deep breaths and tried to stay calm.

Minutes passed before Dennis spoke. His voice was quiet professional. "I don't know anything about nails, I try to keep away from them. Why are you obsessed with nails?"

I mumbled into the pillow. Dennis touched my back and said, "Talk to me. Roll over so I can hear you."

I flipped over to face him. "When Ida went away to visit her grandchildren at Christmas, she gave me keys so I could take care of the bird. I never gave them back. Last night, when I couldn't sleep, I went over there to look around. I haven't been inside since the bombing."

Dennis put his arm around my shoulders and pulled me to his chest. "You shouldn't have done that."

"It was awful." I shuddered, and Dennis hugged me tighter. "It's still a mess. No one's been inside to clean up. Anyway, I went to the kitchen." I stopped; the image of Ida's remains was too vivid to go on.

"What did you find?"

"Nails and a lot of metal pieces that must have come from the bomb. What did you call it the other day?"

"People's shrapnel?"

I nodded. "People's shrapnel—it was scattered all over the floor. I picked up a few pieces and took them to the office today. Remember my story about Eileen's client, the one who died in the fire?"

"I remember. What about the nails?"

I told him about getting one stuck in my shoe and said, "I still have that nail. Dennis, the nails are the same. It has to be the same guy. The two bombs have to be connected...." My voice faded, and I realized how absurd my theory sounded. How many nails were for sale in the city? A million? A billion?

Silence.

Dennis cleared his throat. He gently said, "Blaine, the fire in that grocery store was caused by faulty wiring. The investigators didn't find any bombs. They didn't find anything suspicious. The autopsy said the guy died from smoke inhalation."

"But Dr. Mabe said—"

"I'm telling you what the autopsy said."

"How do you know?"

He sighed. "I wish I was a better liar. Even when I know you're going to be upset, I open my mouth and blurt out the truth."

"You checked up on me?"

"What's the sense of having connections if you don't use them? I was worried about you; I asked around."

I chewed on my lip. "I don't know if I should be angry or flattered. Am I crazy about the nails?"

He kissed my neck. "You're not crazy. You're upset about Eileen and Ida. You're trying too hard to make a connection. You're grasping at straws—or nails."

A fragile silence filled the bedroom. I closed my eyes and listened to his heartbeat. Dennis stroked my hair. "I'll stop by your office tomorrow for those nails. The lab should take a look at them."

We fell asleep wrapped in each other's arms. When I woke again, daylight was coming through the curtains. I turned and reached for Dennis. He was gone. I found my watch under the bed and squinted at it.

Dennis, dressed in another gorgeous suit, walked in carrying a mug of coffee. "Good, you're awake. I don't want to rush you but you're going to be late for work if you don't get out of bed and into the shower."

He put the mug on the bedside table and pushed my legs away to make room for him to sit.

"Dennis, it's only six-thirty." I groaned. "I own the business, no one's going to yell at me if I'm not there at nine."

He kissed me and handed me a ring of keys. "I'm already late, got an early meeting. Lock up when you leave. Keep the keys."

I didn't want to be left alone in his apartment. I didn't want a set of keys. Keys meant commitment. I scrambled from the bed. "Give me five minutes. I'll leave with you." Dennis agreed to wait. He sat on the edge of the bed and drank my coffee while I rushed to dress in stale clothes.

We held hands in the elevator but didn't talk. Dennis was off in another world and I was still half asleep. Another security guard was on duty in front of the television, intently watching cartoons. Dennis greeted him; he grunted without looking up from the screen. We stepped out to the street and walked in opposite directions.

SIXTEEN

I STARTED FOR HOME, confused and guilty. What was I getting into? The "us" Dennis was eager to talk about bothered me. I walked faster, trying to force my mind away from him and back to business. I passed the Y, where thoughts of a ritual cleansing bath came to mind. That silly idea and the hope that Irma would be inside, swimming around with information, propelled me back and up the stairs.

Thanks to Dennis, I beat the morning rush again. The locker room was almost empty. Two women, exercise sessions completed, stood in opposite corners of the room, dressing in dark business suits. I changed and hurried out to the pool.

Irma was pulling herself from the water. She took the towel I held out and wiped her face. "You're lucky—I'm done. How long you gonna be?"

I shrugged. "Depends. How long will you wait? Say the word, I could be done right now."

Irma's brown eyes sparkled. She pointedly looked me over, head to toe, and laughed. "Honey, you need the exercise. I'll give you half an hour, then I'm off."

My leisurely swim turned into a furious session of trying to outswim the many disquieting questions about Dennis, Parker, and Ida. The half hour ended and I didn't have any answers. With leaden arms, I dragged myself from the water and went to the locker room. Irma was lounging on a bench when I walked in panting and wiping my hair with a towel. She found my attempts to catch my breath amusing.

I tossed the wet towel at her head. "Stop laughing. Next time we race, you're dead meat. I'm going to beat your ass."

"Honey, you don't have a prayer." She stopped laughing. "Speaking of dead meat, I casually mentioned your name to my beloved boss last night. Honey, he practically tossed me out of his office."

"What about the gambling?"

Irma's eyes narrowed. "Don't you understand? I don't know if Parker bets on the horses and I ain't gonna ask. I want to get off the overnight, not be buried there for the rest of my natural life."

Another informant down the drain.

"I guess breakfast is out of the question."

"Maybe, maybe not. Who's buying?"

I got stuck with another breakfast tab.

BRAD WAS WAITING in my office, playing with the paperweight from the top of my desk. He looked at me and accusingly said, "You weren't home last night."

I snatched the paperweight from his hands and snapped, "Are you filling in for my mother or my sister? Where I spend the night is none of your business."

"Calm down, Babe. I don't care where you were last night. It couldn't have been much fun or you'd be in a better mood." I blushed, and he laughed. "You told me to call you last night. I gave up around one; I figured you were out for the evening. I've been here since eight-thirty, as ordered, patiently waiting. If we don't hurry, we're going to be late."

I groaned, "Oh God. The memorial service."

Ida's body had been shipped south for interment in her ancestral burial grounds before the neighborhood could acknowledge her death. Seeking to rectify the omission, several of my neighbors organized a ceremony in a nearby church. Dreading their accusing stares, I'd asked Brad to accompany me, counting on his bulk to deter any attacks. Everyone's allowed to act like a coward at times; this was my time.

"I completely forgot. I've been dreading this, everyone together. Everybody knows that package was addressed to me; it's only luck that's kept my name out of the papers. What am I going to do if someone blames me? I don't want to go."

Brad stood and stretched. "No one's going to blame you. If anyone tries, I'll punch him in the nose. If it's a her, I'll punch her too. Come on, Babe, let's get going. You can fill me in on all the juicy gossip in the cab. Start with last night."

NO ONE POINTED AT ME. No one stared at me. No one openly blamed me for Ida's death. We sat near the center of the church. Brad grabbed my hand and kept a tight grip throughout the entire ceremony, occasionally giving it a quiet squeeze of encouragement. I fixed an earnest gaze on the minister and intently followed her movements without hearing a single word.

The service was mercifully brief. When it ended, Brad pulled me to my feet and into the aisle. We joined the slow-moving crowd shuffling to the door. I caught sight of a familiar figure and broke away from Brad, rudely pushing mourners aside, but the man disappeared into the crowd. I made it to the door in time to see him emerge at the bottom of the stairs and walk to a waiting patrol car. I flew down the stairs and grabbed his arm.

"Tony."

"Blaine."

Sparkling conversation. I controlled my surprise and started again. "I didn't expect to see you here. We need to talk."

"Just a curious cop doing his job. I don't have time to shoot the breeze with you, I have a precinct to run."

"You can't just brush me off—"

Brad had finally made his way through the crowd and now hovered behind my shoulder, listening. Parker glanced at him, then back to me.

"Okay, we'll talk. Not here, not now. Tomorrow night, after work. Meet me at my house. Around nine, I'll be home by then." He turned, dove into the car, and slammed the door, narrowly missing my fingers.

Brad waited until the car turned a corner then said, "Reception, office, or hospital? Where do you want to go next?"

"Office." Going to the office was a coward's choice. For the second time that morning, I took it, not eager to face either my neighbors or my sister.

As usual, a pile of messages sat on the top of my desk. I flipped through them and found three from Dennis. Morning-after small talk? I dialed the number; he picked up on the first ring.

Dennis didn't waste time on morning-after pleasantries, and instead jumped right to business. "Who were those people you were with last night at Lloyd's? Did they have anything to do with the bombs?"

Feeling betrayed, I didn't respond.

"Blaine, did you hear me?"

"Halstead. I don't have anything to say to you. Quit meddling in my business."

"So I'm back to being Halstead again. Why won't you trust me? Don't forget, it's my business too. We have a joint task force on terrorism with the NYPD. I plan to talk to some people there, see what they know about your little group."

"Don't do me any favors." My retort was cut off by the loud bang of the office doorknob crashing against the wall. Grammie Blake stood in the doorway, breathing fire. Jona hung behind, futilely trying to hold her back. Dennis's voice buzzed in my ear, and I interrupted his tirade about cooperation. "I have to hang up. Clients are storming my office. Don't go to that task force yet, I'll talk to you later." I hung up and waved Jona away. She backed out and quietly closed the door, leaving me alone with the agitated woman.

Grammie crossed the rug to my desk in three strides and stopped in front of my desk. She turned her purse over and dumped a rusty .38 Special on top of the papers. The gun spun around and came to rest with the barrel pointing at my stomach. I jumped away from the muzzle; she glared at me. "It's not loaded."

Shells cascaded from her hand and rolled across the desk. "It was loaded when I took it from my grand-daughter this morning. I prayed to the Lord for strength and guidance. He sent me to you."

How can you argue with a woman who was sent to you by God? I asked her to sit, picked up the revolver, and swung the cylinder open. The chambers were empty. Despite God's endorsement, I lost my temper. I don't like having guns thrown at me.

"I tried to help and you threw me out. Now you burst into my office, toss a gun on my desk, and scowl at me as if I was the person who gave it to your granddaughter. What do you want from me?"

"Miss Stewart, I am a vain, stupid woman. Please do not turn me away in my time of need. I pray that you find room in your heart to forgive me. Edwina stole my Social Security check to purchase that gun. She wants blood to avenge her father's death. She is determined to kill someone, anyone."

The elderly woman silently recited comforting prayers. If she could pray, I could smoke—we all need our crutches. I lit a cigarette and blew out the match before asking, "Where's Wina?"

"She's in school. I don't know what to do with that girl." Hope lightened the fear in her eyes. "Maybe you will speak with her. Tell Wina you will find her daddy's killer."

"I'll talk to her. Maybe I can convince her that buying guns on the street won't solve her problems, but don't count on it. Wina is a determined young lady. She'll continue to buy guns as long as she thinks it's a solution. If you want me to help, you have to be honest. Your son was involved in a number of illegal activities. Tell me about the papers you burned."

The old woman grimaced and tried to speak. Concerned, I stood up and leaned over the desk. "Mrs. Blake, are you okay? Can I get you a glass of water?"

She gasped and clawed at her chest. Before I could run around the desk, she crumpled to the floor.

"IT WAS A MILD CORONARY." The emergency room doctor peered over the top of his bifocals. "Are you related to this woman?"

I nodded at Wina, who was standing on the opposite side of the corridor, struggling to maintain control. "That's her granddaughter. I'm a friend of the family. What else can you tell me about Mrs. Blake?"

"She's resting comfortably. We might put a pacemaker in to keep things beating properly. We'll decide in a day or two. If you promise to keep the girl quiet, she can see Mrs. Blake for a few minutes. Then she's going to be transferred to a ward. Make sure the girl sees her grandmother now; they don't let children upstairs."

Accustomed to Dr. Mabe's tolerant bedside manner, I pressed for more information. The doctor's face reddened; he impatiently checked his watch and rudely lectured me. "Lady, I have twenty patients to see before my shift ends. The kid's grandmother is in the room at the end of the hall. If you have any more questions, ask a nurse. I don't have time to hold your hand."

The kid didn't like the doctor's attitude and started to tell him. A nurse paused to listen to the exchange. She gently took hold of Wina's arm and pulled her away. "Dr. Harvey's a grouch, but he's a great doctor. Come with me, I'll take you to see your grandmother. She's going to be okay. Try not to look so upset, it'll make her worry." The doctor muttered and stalked away.

I followed Wina and the nurse down the corridor, hanging back when they entered the room. The nurse motioned for me to join them. "Don't leave that girl in there alone; I don't think she can handle herself. Stick your head out if you need anything. I'll be at the station down the hall.''

Grammie's frail body was propped up against the pillows; slow blips moved across the overhead monitor. Wina stared at the screen, hypnotized by the green lines of the measured beats. I fumbled and handed Grammie the purse she had dropped on my carpet. A shaky hand accepted the bag.

She held on to my hand and whispered, ''Bless you. Miss Stewart, I don't have a family. Will you mind Edwina?''

''Grammie, I can mind myself. I don't need nobody to look after me. 'Specially a white—''

''Child, stop.'' The strength of her voice ended Wina's objection—I was too surprised to form one of my own. I was about to become the reluctant custodian of a sixteen-year-old girl who bought guns on her way to school, and I couldn't find a way to object.

The old lady took a deep, rattling breath. ''Child, I'm mighty tired. Go with Miss Stewart—she's a good woman. Mind your manners.'' She closed her eyes and drifted off to sleep. Wina and I stared at each other over the bed; neither one of us was happy with the arrangement.

I murmured, ''Let's go. We'll stop at your house to pick up your clothes, then go to my place.''

Wina opened her mouth and I snapped, ''Don't argue. You're staying with me until your grandmother gets better.''

Our stop at the Blake apartment was brief. Wina sulked in her bedroom, slamming drawers, tossing clothes, books, and sneakers into an overnight bag, muttering curses as she worked. I waited at the kitchen table, sulking and smoking cigarettes. A sixteen-year-old kid: just the thing to make my life perfect.

When we arrived at my house, I pushed my teenage guest into the kitchen and commanded her to sit. The sparse shelves of the refrigerator held a few cans of soda; I handed one to the girl. Wina popped the tab on the can and slouched in a chair. I lit a cigarette and deeply inhaled, trying to enjoy it—the pack was empty and there weren't any more in the house.

Sullen eyes watched me crumple the box and toss it at the garbage can. "You shouldn't smoke, it's bad for you."

"You shouldn't buy guns." I swallowed a mouthful of soda—my petulant guest wasn't impressed. "You don't like this arrangement, neither do I. Just follow my rules and we'll survive. Got it?"

She mumbled into the soda can. I took it for assent and made up a few rules, most of them dealing with school, curfews, and studying. Wina listened without saying a word, then thumped upstairs to the guest bedroom to unpack. I sat at the table and prayed for Grammie's speedy recovery.

It was seven-thirty. I needed a baby-sitter. Brad won the assignment because he was the only person who answered my call. He arrived in less than the half hour he promised, gently cradling a six pack of beer in his arm. I eyed the beer—I hate having alcohol in my house, even if I'm not going to be around when people drink it. I start thinking about how easy it would be to let it back in full-time. I gave Brad a sketchy report of how Wina Blake became a reluctant guest while he drank one of the beers.

"Babe, what the hell are you doing? Investigating a case or playing social worker? You gotta make up your mind. Being scattered is dangerous; you're not focusing."

"Brad, I don't have time to focus—take care of the kid. And don't leave any beer in my refrigerator."

I rushed out of the house and hurried to meet Grant.

SEVENTEEN

I WAS SICK AND TIRED of hanging out in bars. They were all blurring into one indistinguishable mass of smoke, crowds, and pulsating music, and I was finding the craving for a drink increasing with each stop. Vowing that I wouldn't crumble, I walked into the latest bar and searched for Grant without wasting any energy on noticing the patrons or the decor.

Grant was hiding in the shadows of a dark corner, impatiently checking his watch. He watched me approach, raked his fingers through his bushy hair, and smiled. The provocative smile never reached his eyes.

A carafe of red wine was waiting on the table. I pushed a chair back and sat. Despite my seven-hundred-and-fifty-dollar contribution, I had been demoted to the cheap stuff. I pushed the empty wineglass to the center of the table and looked around for a waiter.

My gentleman caller had been replaced by a boor. Grant didn't offer me a drink: he gulped the wine in his glass, refilled it, and ignored me. I shrugged and asked him, "Where's the package? Do you have it with you, or should I pick it up at the office?"

"There won't be a package. Amy was busted this afternoon. Someone on the inside tipped off the cops."

The sour taste of my case falling apart churned in my throat. I frowned. "I'm out, right? Roz is going to use me as a scapegoat. She never wanted me around, she's jealous.''

My response surprised Grant, and he looked puzzled. ''I don't follow you. Why do you think Roz is jealous?''

''Roz is jealous of me, of us. She thinks we have something going. She's been looking for an excuse to get rid of me ever since I walked into her office.''

''You're wrong.''

''I'm right,'' I continued bitterly, hoping Grant's ego would stir. ''Now she's succeeded. Roz won't have to worry about me getting in her way. She got money from me. She doesn't think there's any more, so I'm out.''

''You're out because someone turned. It's too much of a coincidence, a new person gets in and brings the cops along with her. The inner circle made its decision, not me—you're out. It wasn't my decision.'' He pushed his chair back and stood. ''If I thought you were a traitor, you wouldn't have received any warning.''

Grant spun around and marched out, leaving me with the bill. It had been a hell of a day: two tabs, one teenager, one headache. I smoked one last, peaceful cigarette before slowly making my way back home.

Brad was sprawled across the sofa watching a baseball game—one of our home teams was losing again. He greeted me by waving a bottle of beer in the air, and I pushed his feet aside and collapsed.

''Hey, Babe, I hope you had some fun. Things are under control here. The rap queen is upstairs, plotting to overthrow the free world. You know, I think I might go into this baby-sitting business full-time. Babies, beer, and the Bronx Bombers. What a life. Your sister called. She wants to know why you haven't visited her for two days. Want to tell me what's going on around here?''

"It would take too long. Anyway, if I told you, you wouldn't believe me." I closed my eyes and rested my head against the back of the sofa. I felt the weight of Brad's body rise from the sofa and listened to his footsteps across the room. Minutes later, he returned and pressed a cold glass against my cheek.

"Have a soda. Enjoy it, it's the last one. There's nothing left in that refrigerator, Babe. Unless you're into sour milk."

I sat up, took the mug of soda from his hand, and groaned. "I forgot to stop to buy milk and bread and stuff. What the hell am I going to feed that kid in the morning?"

"That's why God made coffee shops. Take her out, teach her to read a menu. Let me try the question again. What's going on?"

I put the mug down on top of some magazines scattered across the end table and looked around the room. It needed a thorough cleaning. I had a brief, envious thought of Dennis and his cleaning man. Brad impatiently tapped his feet—he wasn't going to be diverted by a discussion of my lack of housekeeping skills.

"Everything fell apart. I don't know what happened. Yesterday, I was making progress. Tonight, my cover's semi-blown and I'm not sure there's enough left to salvage. The kid got a gun and gave her grandmother a heart attack. The grandmother gave me the kid. And I haven't called Eileen because she's going to bitch at me."

"Sounds bad, Babe. Want some advice?"

"No. Answers I'll take. Advice I don't need." I sighed. "Brad, I'm sorry. If you don't mind, I'm going to throw you out. I'm going to take a bath and go to bed. Maybe I'll skip the bath and just go to bed."

Brad grinned. "No problem, I've known you too long to be offended when you toss me out. I'll catch you in the morning. I cancelled a hot date so I could baby-sit for you. I'm going to try to warm her up."

He left. I watched the Yankees blow the game for good in the ninth because of a fielding error and decided to crawl into bed. My plan was to hide under the covers until morning.

I couldn't sleep. Every creak and groan whispered by the old house instantly snapped me awake, sending me groping in the dark for my gun. All the problems I'd been trying to avoid rushed into my head. I tried punching the pillows and tossing and turning but my haunted thoughts wouldn't go away.

My cigarettes were in the living room. I rolled out of bed, put on a robe in case my houseguest was wandering around, and went down to the living room to sit, smoke, and wait for exhaustion to overwhelm me. After two puffs, I realized I didn't want another cigarette. I stubbed it out and sat in the dark, too exhausted to move.

The light on the answering machine in the hallway was blinking. I watched it, the modern equivalent of ashes glowing in the hearth, until curiosity pulled me from the rocking chair.

Two blinks, two messages. The first was a computer trying to sell me life insurance. My machine had clicked off in the middle of the robosales pitch. The second was a woman's voice delivering a short message: "You need more exercise. Try swimming. Tomorrow. Eight-thirty."

I forced a yawn, trying to convince myself I was ready to sleep. I went back to the living room and fell asleep on the sofa.

EIGHTEEN

THE REALITY of the hell of my overnight acquisition of a sixteen-year-old girl hit at six forty-five.

The creepy feeling of being watched woke me from a restless, uncomfortable sleep. I forced my eyelids open. Wina's unhappy face was inches away, a faint streak of sunlight glinting off the diamond stud in her nostril. I rubbed my eyes, wondering what rabbit hole I had fallen through.

"Why you sleeping here?" Without waiting for an answer, she morosely said, "You got nothing to eat. Grammie always cooks breakfast for me."

The muscles in my back yelped when I moved—I was too old to spend the night on a sofa that was on its way to being lumpy. I yawned and cautiously stretched. "I'm not your Grammie. It's been about two weeks since I've been shopping. Give me half an hour to get dressed. I'll take you out for breakfast." She frowned. I snapped, "Don't make faces. Go get dressed." My pre-coffee meanness overpowered Wina's attitude. She thumped up the stairs, and I dragged behind to loosen my stiff back in a hot shower.

Exactly twenty-three minutes later, I dragged myself back down the stairs. Wina was sitting in the rocking chair, Walkman clamped over her ears, impatiently rocking back and forth. We made an odd (even by Greenwich Village standards) procession down Barrow Street to a coffee shop on Sixth Avenue.

Remembering my mother's old, inaccurate warnings about not swimming on a full stomach, I drank coffee and smoked a cigarette. Wina devoured eggs with all the trimmings. She looked at my cigarette and attempted to deliver another antismoking lecture.

I rolled my eyes. "Why don't you worry about your own health? Stop buying guns, you'll live longer."

Wina snarled, "You can't stop me. I'm going to find the motherfucker who killed my father and kill him."

"Where are you getting the guns?"

Wina shook her head and concentrated on using a piece of toast to push the last bits of scrambled egg onto the fork. She stuffed the egg into her mouth, popped the toast in on top of it, and mumbled, "Worry 'bout your own damn business." The sight of food rolling around the inside of her mouth turned my stomach, and I looked away. Wina finished her sentence by calling me a bitch. It was too early to fight, so I shrugged and deliberately lit another cigarette. I silently said another prayer for Grammie's speedy recovery.

We finished breakfast in ill-humored silence and, glad to escape from each other, walked off in different directions. Wina headed to school, I strolled to the Y.

Irma was already in the pool. I watched her swim a few laps, then turned back to the locker room. Doing laps with churning coffee burning a hole in my stomach was more than I could bear. I slipped into the whirlpool, closed my eyes, and relaxed in the warm, bubbling water.

A wet towel lightly flicked across my face, and I snapped awake. Irma wrapped the towel around her shoulders and laughed. "Afraid to try your luck against me today?"

"It's too early for comedy. You called me—what do you want?"

"Word got to Parker that I was breaking bread with you. He spent twenty minutes reaming me out for sneaking around behind his back. You're in deep shit with my boss and I don't want to be dragged down with you. Find yourself another girl."

Irma turned and hurried away before Parker's spies spotted her talking to me. I gave Irma enough time to get out of the locker room before scrambling out of the tub to dress and finish demolishing my day—I was going to visit my sister.

Eileen was home, discharged the previous day, the momentous occasion marred by my absence. Or so she told me.

Three times, I listened to her rebukes, a new record for me. Three times, I clamped my lips together and smiled. The fourth time, desperate to change to another subject, I interrupted.

"How's your eye? I haven't heard any reports lately."

"The right one's gone. The other's coming back. Dr. Mabe says it should take about a month. She's wrong; I'll be back in the office next week."

Eileen's blithe tone astonished me. Put in the same position, I would have been a raving maniac, requiring massive doses of tranquilizers. I started another question but she wouldn't let me finish.

"I'm sure the office is a wreck. You never pay enough attention to the details. What about the billing? Is it up-to-date?"

I forced a smile and allowed Eileen to drift back to complaining. "Where were you yesterday? Everyone else managed to get here."

"Give it a rest, Eileen. I'm sorry I missed your party—I was working. And the office is fine. I'm more than capable of keeping it going." I regained control of my temper and grinned. "Lighten up, we're making money."

No reaction. Eileen wasn't listening; she was staring across the room at nothing. I tried a different approach. "If you don't want to talk about your problems, let's talk about mine. I have plenty—my case is falling apart. Faradeux is going to blow when he hears I haven't made any progress since his call. And my teenage guest called me a bitch at breakfast."

"I don't want to listen. I don't want to talk. I'm going to make tea."

Eileen stood. Grabbing at the furniture and walls for balance, she made her way down the hallway to the kitchen with shaky, carefully placed steps. I watched and thought about following but decided to stay in the living room. Checking up on Eileen would cause a war.

I picked up the *Times* and scanned the editorials, telling myself to loosen up—Eileen would work it out. She'd get back to normal without my constant lecturing. Eileen always gave me good advice: I was confident she would follow her own counsel.

A loud crash sent me running to the kitchen. Eileen was leaning against the kitchen table, sobbing hysterically. The remains of a mug, a teakettle, and a puddle of water formed a neat circle in front of the stove.

"Eileen, it's no big deal. Just a little mess, easy to clean up." I tried to put a comforting arm around her shoulders, but Eileen hiccuped and thrust my hand away.

"Leave me alone.... I can hardly see out of this damn eye—the good one. What a joke. What am I going to do? I can't even make a cup of tea."

"Eileen—"

"Leave me alone. Get out of here. Just leave me alone."

She continued her temper tantrum. I took a dustpan from the cabinet beneath the sink and started to clean. Eileen drooped in a chair, sniffling as she tried to regain control.

"Eileen, you have to talk about this. Learn to deal with it and get on with your life."

She lashed out. "I don't need your preaching. What the hell do you know?"

I know enough about getting on with life to fill a set of encyclopedias, but Eileen wasn't ready to listen. Stubbornness runs in the family. I ignored her and swept up the mess, occasionally glancing over my shoulder. She didn't move or acknowledge my presence.

Wanting a drink stronger than tea, I made more tea, filled two mugs, and carried them to the table. Eileen cradled the mug between her hands and cautiously brought it to her lips. Wincing at the sight of my fiercely independent sister appearing so vulnerable, I looked away.

Praying that the day wouldn't get worse, I walked back to my office. When I walked into the lobby and saw Dennis sitting in the lobby, I smiled. Maybe the day was going to improve. Dennis didn't notice me; he was busy scowling at the front page of the *Wall Street Journal*. I sat down next to him and pulled the paper away from his face.

"Dennis, I didn't expect to see you sitting here. Did you come to take me to lunch?"

He frowned and said, "I'm here on business. Can we go to your office? We have to talk."

My stomach lurched—a clear signal that the day was about to get much worse. I got to my feet and silently led the grim procession to my office. I kept glancing at Dennis but his bleak face didn't give a hint of what was wrong. Anticipating an unpleasant encounter, my stomach tightened painfully.

Jona waved a stack of messages at me. As usual, I ignored them, and led Dennis into my office. He dropped his rumpled newspaper on my desk and walked over to the windows. I closed the door and turned to face him.

"Dennis?" He didn't answer. I took a deep breath and spoke to his back. "What's wrong? You look...I don't know. I've never seen you look so grim."

"I've been reassigned. The investigation into the bombings has been closed."

I flew across the room and grabbed Dennis's arm. "Tell me you're making a bad joke. How can the investigation be closed? You showed me the lab report. Are you just going to ignore it?''

He pushed my hand off his arm and glared at me. After a few seconds, he spoke in a carefully controlled monotone. "The order came from way over my head. The investigation is a waste of agency resources. The bomb in Ida's kitchen wasn't a bomb; it was a gas explosion. You think it's a bomb because you're distraught, upset by the attack on your sister. A disgruntled client sent that bomb. A warrant is out to arrest Rudy MacIntyre."

I was too angry to hear the message behind his emotionless voice. "Is that why you were waiting for me? To tell me that the FBI has decided I'm a hysterical female who's just a little bit paranoid?"

"Let me explain—"

I wasn't going to give him a chance to explain anything. I yelled, "Forget it, I don't want to listen to your phony excuses. Thanks, Dennis. I really appreciate your support."

"Stop yelling. Listen to me."

My office has thick walls so I wasn't worried about anyone overhearing. Without lowering my voice, I said, "I don't want to listen to you. You blew it, Dennis. You gave up."

Dennis flushed and raised his voice to match mine. "Didn't you hear me? The order came from way over my head."

I wanted to slap him. I even lifted my hand, but stopped. Slapping Dennis would only make the situation worse. I forced my hands into my pockets and shook my head.

"You're pitiful. If I gave up as often as you do, I'd be collecting welfare. You delivered your message, now get out of here. I've got a lot of work to do."

Dennis touched my chin and turned my face to his. "Don't go nuts on me. Just listen to me for a few seconds before you throw me out. It's very hard for us mere mortals to meet your high standards, but I'm trying. I'm not abandoning you. I know Ida was killed by a bomb. I also know that bomb was meant for you. But I can't ignore an order from my boss."

I pushed his hand away. "Great—keep your boss happy. Make me happy too, leave me alone."

"You are—"

"If you call me an idiot again, I'm going to smack you."

Dennis smiled. "Then let me finish before you start yelling. My boss can't tell me what to do after hours. A lot of people owe me favors and I'm going to call them all in. Damn it, Blaine, I'm on your side. I'm not going to leave you hanging. When are you going to start trusting me?"

The conversation was getting out of control, into territory I didn't want to explore. I took a step back and looked away from Dennis's eyes. He softly repeated, "When?"

I didn't answer. He walked out of the room, carefully closing the door behind him.

NINETEEN

A TERSE MESSAGE from Parker sat on my desk: "Meeting cancelled." No explanation, just a simple "Meeting cancelled."

I tried calling; the noncommittal voice answering the phone promised to leave a message. Disgusted after three attempts, I gave up and spent the rest of the day in front of the computer, burying my worries about Eileen and my crumbling cases in routine paperwork, and doing my best to keep my boasts truthful about making money despite Eileen's absence. Dennis's parting comment rattled around inside my head all afternoon. It bothered me—but not enough to make me pick up the phone.

Brad strolled in around five and tossed a thin file on my desk. "Here it is, Babe, everything you asked for. The guys did a great job."

The guys, male and female, are our skip tracers, people who have perfected the art of acquiring information about anyone. Their tools are simple—give the skip tracer a telephone and a question and they'll find the answer. It's easy. People will give out an amazing amount of information over the phone—if you know how to ask for it. Skip tracers know how to ask. They're chameleons who change their voices, slang, and personalities to match the person on the other end of the line. Clerks think they're talking to clerks, supervisors to supervisors, accountants to accountants, company presidents to company presidents.

Skip tracers collect and protect their sources, carefully guarding their identities and nurturing their relationships, until a single phone call can uncover data that would take me weeks to unearth. We employ a roomful of the best; they're worth every cent we pay for salaries, coffee, and cigarettes. Skip tracers always smoke.

"They did a slow job. I asked for this a week ago. I'm running out of time."

"Hey, Babe, go easy. The guys have been working hard on this. They ran every scam in the book and invented a few more to get this."

I kept my eyes fixed on an uncooperative column of figures that wouldn't balance. "What does your little file say? I don't have time to read."

Brad sat and made himself comfortable. I heard the plunk of shoe leather hitting the top of my desk. Brad ignored the frown I sent over my shoulder, tipped the chair back on its hind legs, and started reciting.

"Grant Wilder: Forty-one years old, lives in Brooklyn with Rosalynn Carter. He draws a small salary from WARM, no other visible source of income."

"What about the military? He told me he lost his fingers in Vietnam."

"Wilder did a tour of duty in '68. Listen to this, Babe: he was in the Special Forces, munitions expert. He came back, enrolled at Columbia, and spent the rest of the war years protesting the war."

"What about the rest of them?"

"Rosalynn was a year behind at Columbia, that's where they met. Rosalynn was also active in the anti-war movement. The story is that she and Grant were in with some pretty radical folks. After 'Nam was over, they drifted around, terrorists without a cause. I don't know when they got into the animal rights business, but they had to find something to protest—we haven't had a good war since Vietnam, all the others end too soon."

"Forget the political commentary, Brad, I'm not interested. Just give me facts."

"Okay, Babe, no politics. We don't have anything on Hodgkins yet."

The computer screen was giving me a headache. I turned to face Brad and lit a cigarette. "Why not?"

Brad shrugged. "They were concentrating on the other two. WARM is a new organization, incorporated a year ago. Their bank account is generally low; the balance is under a thousand. Lots of small deposits with an occasional large one. Give us three, four days, we'll have copies of their statements."

"I don't have three or four days. I need to know who's giving money to WARM and how it's being spent. Tomorrow, Brad. I need to know tomorrow."

In one fluid movement, Brad swung his feet from my desk and stood, surprisingly graceful for a man carrying 275 pounds of solid muscle. He saluted. "You got it. Tomorrow. Nobody goes home until you have all the answers."

I muttered, "I wish it was that easy to get all the answers." Brad laughed and walked out to give his crew the bad news about working late.

Cigarette in hand, I turned back to the computer and tried to force my mind to work. It was impossible. Thoughts of Dennis kept intruding.

I tried to file him in the back of my mind for later examination but he wouldn't stay there. "When are you going to start trusting me?" kept rattling around inside my head. At six o'clock I finally admitted defeat and grabbed the phone to ask Dennis to meet me later in the evening, after I took care of some casework. He agreed. It would soon be time to confront Dennis and my fears.

POKER FANS KNOW ALL about the art of bluffing—misleading the other players and raising the size of the pot while holding a hand of lousy cards. I walked into WARM's suite, holding lousy cards and wondering if they could spot a bluff. My idea, and it wasn't a very good one, was my last attempt to buy my way in.

Roz and Grant were sitting at the table. They jumped, startled by my sudden invasion. I yanked an envelope from my pocket and flipped it onto the table between them.

"Take it, don't be stupid. I have a few things to say."

Practical Grant opened the envelope and ruffled the bills with his thumb. When Roz started to interrupt, he snapped, "Let Blaine finish."

"Amy was busted for buying cocaine from an undercover cop, not because someone in the group turned her in. The woman doesn't have any sense; she has a habit of buying from cops."

"How did you—"

I laughed. "Roz, I have great sources. Your Faradeux protest is in trouble. I can help."

Grant slid the envelope across the table to Roz. A stack of bills spilled out, quieting any objections she was planning to make.

"How can you help us?"

Imitating all the bad private-eye movies I had ever watched on television, I rested my hands on the table and leaned over them. Neither one snickered at my late-show lines.

"Nonhumans will never be given the right to live without exploitation. We have to seize those rights for them. I'm ready to fight."

Harold Hodgkins walked in and glared at me; I cursed myself for not locking the door. Roz snatched the money from the table and quickly stuffed it into the envelope. She dropped the package to her lap, afraid I'd change my mind and take it back. Unable to hide his curiosity, Hodgkins stared at me as he removed papers from his briefcase.

Grant squeezed my arm. "You'd better go. I'll call you later."

No one was interested in continuing the discussion. I left, two thousand dollars poorer. I tried listening at the door; it was too thick. My great plan disintegrated. I viciously punched the elevator button, and the doors glided apart.

Grant rushed from the office and held the elevator doors open. "Blaine, wait—"

"I don't have any more money."

"The things you said in there, were you serious?"

"Of course I was serious. Do you think I threw two thousand dollars on the table for fun?" I shook my head. "You people are lunatics."

"We aren't lunatics. We're cautious. If you're willing and ready to fight, we can use you. Are you in?"

I nodded. Grant smiled. "Good. Meet me tomorrow morning at the Stock Exchange. I'll be in the visitors' gallery at eleven. Don't come earlier—the guards get nervous if you hang around too long."

IT WAS GOING ON NINE when I left Chelsea. If my old boss hadn't changed his old habits, he would be finishing a solitary dinner at the Italian restaurant a block away from his apartment building. Then he would walk home, smoking a cigar along the way. I planned to ambush him in the hallway of his apartment building.

Sweet-talking my way past the indifferent doorman wasn't difficult—he was more interested in the Racing Form than screening visitors. I gave him five bucks for the horses, told him I wanted to surprise a friend, and walked to the elevator. I went up to Parker's floor and lounged on his doorstep, smoking cigarettes and counting the floor tiles.

A door at the end of the hallway opened, and an elderly woman popped her head out and nearsightedly peered at me. I made a face at her—I didn't want to get involved with any more little old ladies; they cause too much heartache. My effort was lost in her myopic haze. Deciding I wouldn't do too much damage on a cop's doorstep, she slammed the door, and the clicking of lock tumblers echoed down the hallway.

Parker bypassed the elevator and climbed the stairs, cautiously stepping out from behind the stairwell door. He saw me and sheepishly tucked his service revolver into the pocket of his suit jacket.

"The guy downstairs told me somebody snuck past him and stopped on my floor. Dumb bastard, if he had bothered to look up from his paper, he would have been able to describe you. Would have saved me the trouble of climbing all those stairs. I'm getting too old for this shit." Parker was having trouble catching his breath and was working hard to hide it.

"You should trash those cigars and get more exercise. Aren't you going to ask me in?"

Tony's eyes narrowed, trying to calculate how much noise I'd make if he refused. He wisely decided the risk was too great. He unlocked the door and grudgingly let me inside.

Recently divorced after twenty-three years of a marriage that had produced three sons, all cops, and a tired, bitter wife who had finally given up, Parker was left with the apartment and the remains of his marriage. The apartment hadn't changed much since my last visit two years before. Scrape a layer of dust from the furniture and the apartment would look as if his wife had never left. I wondered if Parker missed her for anything other than cooking and cleaning.

"Let's sit in the kitchen. The rest of the place is a mess."

I nodded and followed Parker to the only clean room in the house. Without asking, he poured scotch into two glasses. He put one down before me, drained the other, and quickly refilled it. He then placed the bottle in the center of the table and sat.

I pushed the glass away and asked, "I don't suppose you have a soda hidden in that refrigerator, do you?"

"Shit, I forgot you don't drink." Parker pulled the glass to him. "No sense in letting this go to waste. Sorry, kid, no soda. I guess you're here because I backed out on you for tonight. What's so important that you had to park yourself on my doorstep?"

He stuck a cigar in his mouth, held a match to it, and puffed. Flames spurted out, giving a pretty good imitation of a fire-breathing dragon.

"I've been hearing things about you, Tony, things that worry me. I wanted to hear it from your mouth."

"You know how cops love to gossip. You shouldn't pay attention to all the garbage you hear." Another cloud of smoke rolled across the table. "So tell me, what bad stuff have you been hearing?"

"Things like putting the word out that your cops shouldn't talk to me. What about closing down the investigation into Hurley Blake's death? And how did you pull the FBI off the bomb that killed my neighbor?"

Parker tapped some nonexistent ash into the ashtray and sipped his whiskey. "Is that what's wrong? The way you look, eyes wild, hair flying all over the place, I thought something awful had happened. You gotta ignore the scuttlebutt around the station—nothing's going on. Look, kid, I'm flattered that you think I'm so powerful, but I don't have clout with the Feds. The FBI must have a good reason for dropping the case. Maybe there isn't anything to investigate."

"Tony, I saw the lab reports on the bomb in Ida's kitchen. Overnight, a bomb becomes a gas explosion.

Do you expect me to believe that? Why are you telling your people to stay away from me?''

"I haven't shut anything down. I warned my people away from you because I'm trying to protect you. I don't want you to get hurt." He puffed on the cigar. "I heard you turned the guy you thought bombed your sister and you're getting your information from him."

"MacIntyre—who told you about him?"

Parker smiled. I realized my mistake—too late to pull it back.

"That's what I heard. Now who you gonna believe, an ex-con or your old sarge? Come on, Blaine, I'm on your side."

"Let's talk about something else. What's going to happen to the fancy assignment you're after when word gets out that you owe money to the bookies?"

The expression on Parker's face sent me searching my memory for CPR instructions. But the heart attack didn't happen. Tony leaned toward me, and angry clouds of smoke streamed from the cigar.

"I should throw your smart ass out of here. Who do you think you are? What gives you the right to sit in my house and make snide accusations?"

"I thought we were friends. You were at my wedding. You were on the team with my husband when he got killed."

"Who told you that? I never told you that...."

DENNIS ARRIVED on my doorstep minutes after I got home. I barely had time to kick off my shoes and socks, pay the baby-sitter—a neighborhood college student who looked mean enough to keep Wina in

line—and check on my sleeping guest before the
doorbell rang. I hurried to the door, regretting the
impulsive invitation I'd made a few hours earlier. I
didn't want to get involved in a heart-to-heart with
Dennis, I wanted to douse my aching head with cold
water and collapse on the sofa.

Dennis had gotten rid of his suit and tie; he was
dressed in faded jeans and an old rugby shirt. I recognized the shirt. It had been a birthday present—the
only gift he'd ever received from me. By the time the
holidays came around, we had already split. I stared
at the shirt, remembering the lunch hours I'd given up
to shop for the perfect present.

Dennis cleared his throat. "Can I come in? Or are
you going to slam the door in my face? Remember,
you invited me."

His voice startled me back to real time. I took a deep
breath and said, "Sorry. That shirt brings back a lot
of memories."

"The memories are good. It's the present that gives
us trouble." He smiled. "Can I come in, please? I
promise to behave myself."

I hesitated, then swung the door wide open. There
would be no casual dismissals this evening. Dennis had
come to do business.

We settled in the living room. I quickly sat in the
rocking chair near the fireplace, leaving the sofa to
Dennis. He knew why I'd chosen that chair and didn't
like it.

"What's gotten into you? A few nights ago you
climbed into bed with me without any fear. Tonight
you won't even sit next to me. I don't understand
you."

I ran my fingers through my hair and rocked back in the chair. "You're not alone. I don't understand myself. My trust receptors have short-circuited. Alarms keep going off when I'm with you or Tony—people I know I should trust. Everything's been turned upside down. I have a teenager that I don't like sleeping upstairs. Ida's dead. Eileen's . . . Eileen's hiding in her kitchen, making believe nothing's wrong. I'm stuck in a mad, dark whirlwind. And I'm afraid it's all because I missed something." I stood up abruptly. "I want a cigarette—be right back."

I wanted more than a cigarette, I wanted peace. But Dennis was waiting and he wasn't going to quietly disappear into the night. I rummaged unsuccessfully through the kitchen cabinets before finally finding an unopened pack of cigarettes in the refrigerator.

Dennis hadn't moved from the sofa. When I walked into the room he held out a hand and said, "Why don't you sit here? This sofa is much more comfortable than that rickety old rocking chair."

"That chair is an antique. And it isn't rickety."

Dennis laughed. "If you sit next to me, I'll answer every question you ask."

I was too tired to argue, too tired to think about my feelings. I plopped down next to Dennis and let him light my cigarette. After taking a deep drag, I exhaled and asked, "What about the investigation?"

"I've never seen anything like it. We were barely operational when the plug was pulled." Dennis tried to keep his voice neutral—he almost succeeded. "I know you think I gave up but you're wrong. I'm still trying to work on it but I have to be quiet about it. Fighting will only get me transferred to some remote outpost. You can't say I quit, but you can say I'm selfish—I want to hang around here."

"But—" I was going to ask how the evidence could be ignored but I knew the question was naive. Evidence can always be ignored. I sighed. "Forget it."

"Forget what? You're running away from me again." He nodded at the cigarette in my hand. "You got your cigarettes. What excuse are you going to use now to disappear?"

"Give me a minute, I'll think of something." Dennis frowned. I quickly said, "Smile, that's a joke, son."

"Before you run away again, why don't you tell me about your day? Maybe we can make some sense out of this mess."

I repeated my conversation with Parker and the surprise ending. In the quiet that followed, I leaned forward to light another cigarette. When I sat back, Dennis put his arm around my shoulders and asked, "So, what do you think?"

"It was a weird reaction. I didn't remember he was on that team until I read Jeff's old notebooks." I shrugged. "He said he's trying to protect me. I wish he'd stop, I don't need protection."

Dennis shifted his arm to a more comfortable position around my shoulders and stroked my hair. "What happened after that?"

"He picked up his cigar and threw me out."

This was the perfect time to tell Dennis about my other meeting—the one with WARM—and my plan to meet Grant in the morning. The little voice inside that gives advice, sometimes good, sometimes bad, stopped me; I wasn't ready to push this trust business too far. I yawned. "I'm going to bed. Are you staying?"

"Do you want me to stay?"

Without hesitation, I answered. "Yes."

Later, after Dennis finally drifted to sleep, I found myself staring at the ceiling, arms folded beneath my head, worrying about domestic matters. The refrigerator was still empty, and my hungry houseguests would be up in a few hours demanding breakfast. Smiling at my concern about household issues, I fell asleep.

A rude hand shook me awake. I buried my face in the pillow and mumbled, "Leave me alone."

"Get up, I'm hungry. I already looked in your refrigerator. You don't have any food so you have to take us out for breakfast."

Without opening my eyes, I groped for a pillow, found one, and tossed it over my shoulder at Dennis. He didn't go away.

"If you don't get up, I'll let the rap queen in here. I bet that kid can be incredibly rude in the morning."

I giggled. "Yo, bitch, get out of bed. I demand to be fed." I rolled over, convinced my eyes to open, and squinted at him. "Why are you doing this to me?"

"Because I love you. Because I'm hungry."

I groaned. "It's too early. I can't love a man who wakes me at the crack of dawn and doesn't bring me coffee. I need coffee."

Dennis bent to kiss me, briefly diverting his attention from his rumbling stomach. "Let's make a deal. I'll make coffee. I'll also be sure the kid is awake. You"—he kissed me again—"have to get out of bed."

I lied and agreed; I had no intention of getting out of bed. As soon as he left the room, I grabbed all the pillows and burrowed into them for another half hour of sleep. The bedroom door opened, and I jammed a pillow over my head to muffle Dennis's reproach.

"Get up." The playful tone had disappeared from his voice. "The kid's gone. The bed was slept in but she's not in the house. I checked around outside. She's gone."

"Let her go." I swept the pillows and sheet to the floor, sat up, looked around for my clothes, and started complaining. Complaining always wakes me up. "I want to live alone again. I like living alone. Maybe she left for school."

"It's six-thirty, a little early for school. Her books are still in the bedroom. What do you want me to do?"

"Find my sneakers."

Yesterday's jeans and blouse were draped over the chair near the window where I'd thrown them the night before. They'd be good enough for hunting a missing child; I quickly pulled them on. From across the room, Dennis tossed running shoes at me. Outfit complete. I grabbed money and housekeys, stuffed everything into my pockets, and looked at Dennis.

He was showered, shaved, and dressed. He was wide awake, which infuriated me: no one should be awake and alert at six-thirty in the morning.

"Let's go. When I find her, I'm going to kill her."

"Where are we going?"

"The coffee shop. If she isn't there, we'll get coffee and try her apartment. Then the school. Then the hospital. After that, I give up."

The coffee shop was empty. Dennis glanced at his watch. Pleading an early meeting, he dropped out of the search. Understanding his reluctance to get involved in my domestic problems, I watched him disappear into the subway station, then hurried across town.

TWENTY

ALL THE NEIGHBORHOOD junkies and beggars were out on Avenue B enjoying the sunshine and asking passersby for money. My mood was too foul to consider charity. I ignored their curses when I refused and kept walking.

A freshly shattered lock hung uselessly at the lobby door. I pushed through and stepped inside. A bored janitor was spreading disinfectant around the floor, mixing the fresh pine scent with stale odors lingering from the previous evening's dinners. I tiptoed around the puddles and sprinted up the stairwell.

The fifth-floor hallway was quiet. I groped in my pocket for the key ring I had lifted from Grammie's purse during the wild ambulance ride, and let myself in. Justifying my snooping with the need to find Wina, I began to search the cramped rooms.

Her room was first. It was a typical teenager's room, cluttered with textbooks, discarded clothes, cassettes, makeup, posters of musicians, and jewelry. I poked through the closet, then turned to the desk.

No diary, no list of friends or hiding places. I found several bullets—but no gun—three condoms, and a yellowing snapshot. The bullets and the condoms didn't hold any interest. The picture did. I slipped it into my back pocket and crossed the hall to Grammie's bedroom.

Her room was a vivid contrast to the chaos across the hall. It was spotless. Religious icons followed me with disapproving eyes as I opened drawers and pushed aside the dresses in the closet until the sterile emptiness and overpowering feelings of voyeurism overcame me. I gave up and left the flat.

With dragging feet, I walked the forty-five blocks to the hospital where Grammie Blake was a patient, using the time to rehearse stories of how I lost Wina. They all sounded feeble. The morning's only bright spot came at the hospital: Grammie was sleeping. My coward's heart lightened—I had another day before facing the woman who had entrusted her granddaughter to my incompetent care.

AFTER LOSING QUARTERS in four different phone booths, I gave up on trying to check in with the office and flagged down a taxi. If my meager thread of luck held, I'd make it to the financial district with enough time for a bagel and coffee.

There's a small museum in the lobby of the visitors' gallery; I didn't stop to look at the exhibits. I shoved through the crowd to the gallery. Grant was standing at the far end of the narrow balcony overlooking the trading floor, watching the activity below his feet.

A thick pane of glass, added after demonstrators once showered dollar bills on the floor, enclosed the balcony. Trading had stopped briefly when the money fluttered to the floor, and everyone had abandoned their posts in a mad scramble for the cash. The glass went up the next day.

I greeted Grant, moved slightly so his kiss landed on my cheek, and looked down at the floor. The summer doldrums had struck a full month before the summer solstice, slowing trading to lazy August levels. Traders stood in small clumps around their stations, gossiping and telling jokes.

"Look at them. Greedy bastards. Capitalist whores. Selling out..."

Childish slogans poured from Grant's mouth. Without listening, I nodded in agreement, wondering if he was capable of a prolonged conversation that didn't contain revolutionary clichés.

"...your money will be put to good use." I pulled my attention back to Grant. He was pointing to the metal scaffolding hanging from the ceiling, holding computer cables, telephone wires, and power lines to the booths where trades were executed. "The bombs are going in those rafters. A timer will detonate them at exactly nine-thirty on Monday morning, when Faradeux hits the gong." He smiled. "Do you like how we're spending your money?"

I didn't. A pack of tourists stopped beside me. I waited until they moved out of earshot before answering. "Overhead bombs won't cause much damage. Couldn't the placement be better?"

"The inner circle has made its decision. I have to follow it, even if I don't agree. Instead of blowing the fuckers up, like they deserve, we'll shower them with red paint, symbolizing the blood being shed by innocent nonhumans."

I grabbed the wooden railing for support and clamped my mouth down on hysterical laughter. "Red paint? I thought..."

Grant's voice was muffled by the overhead speakers murmuring facts about the Exchange. I moved closer to hear him. "I've been thinking, maybe we can really surprise them."

MARCELLA HALFHEARTEDLY held out a stack of messages as I walked in the door. The expression on my face had already warned her that I wasn't interested. I rushed past her outstretched hand to my office. I didn't care who was on the phone or who was waiting to see me, I needed to think.

Brad stopped me and waved a yellow sheet of paper in front of my face. "Hey, Babe, I've been looking for you. Jeannie called the bank and cried a little. Said she was WARM's new bookkeeper and was going to get fired because she lost the statement. Some clerk who identifies with miserable bosses was happy to read the information to her. No checks made payable to Bombs-R-Us. No deposits from a Faradeux child." He gave me the paper and said, "Sorry, Babe. No smoking gun."

I glanced at the neat handwritten columns on the sheet. One was labeled "Deposits," the other "Withdrawals"; none of the names in either column were recognizable. I folded the paper and looked at Brad. "Thank Jeannie. Tell the other guys thanks, too. I know they've been working hard. Friday after work, drinks are on me."

"Okay. I'll set it up. Hey, what do you think about Eileen?"

I shrugged. "I haven't talked to Eileen—I'm not sure we're talking at all. We used her kitchen as a battleground the other day. She cursed me out, then tossed me out.''

Brad smiled. Annoyed by the smug look on his face, I growled, ''What are you laughing at?''

''Nothing.''

Brad shifted away, attempting to escape. I hung on to his arm.

''Nothing, Babe. Relax, you're too jumpy. Your nerves are shot. Go home, get a good night's sleep.''

He pulled away and sprinted down the corridor. I yelled after him, ''Brad, come back here.''

''Later, Babe. I got work to do, stuff you've been nagging me about.''

''Brad.'' He waved over his shoulder and disappeared around a corner. Feeling like Rodney Dangerfield, I walked into my office muttering, ''All I want is a little respect. No one listens to me....''

A woman was sitting behind my desk, holding a paper inches from her face, struggling to read the type. She dropped the paper and looked at me. ''I listen. It may take a day or two for me to realize you were right, but I do listen to you.''

The patch over Eileen's right eye, color coordinated to match her suit, added a bizarre touch to her chatter. A Don't-touch / Don't-ask-questions look was set on her face. I stared at her, unsure of what to say. I decided to go with the obvious question. ''What are you doing here?''

''What have you been up to this morning?''

We spoke at the same time. Eileen laughed. ''Me first, my answer's shorter. I decided to listen to you and get back to work. Where have you been? Talk fast, your Faradeux pals are due here in about three minutes.''

I groaned. ''When did they call? I wasn't expecting them until tomorrow.''

''Jacob won the first-caller-of-the-day award.'' Everyone in my office hates the first caller of the day—it's usually an irate client, or an irate potential client. ''Jacob insisted he had to meet with you this morning. Where have you been this morning? I assume it's related to Faradeux.''

Eileen listened to my story of Grant and his red paint bombs. She put her head back and chuckled. ''Perfect! Faradeux will be so happy; you solved his case a few days early. He can have his big party without worrying about the nasty protestors.'' I folded my arms across my chest and stared at my feet. Eileen stopped laughing and leaned across the desk to peer at my face.

''What's wrong? You should be happy. It's over; grab Dennis and go away for a few days.''

''This isn't over yet. Here, look at this.'' I gave Eileen the picture from Wina's desk. ''The guy on the right is Hurley Blake. Grant Wilder is the one in the middle with his arm around Blake. Wilder served in Vietnam, Special Forces. I guess Blake did too.''

Eileen studied the picture carefully. After a few seconds, I asked, ''If you're going to blow something up, where's the best place to get the explosives? How about an old army buddy who specializes in black market weapons?''

I lit a cigarette and took a series of short, angry pulls on it, sending the smoke out over Eileen's head. ''I called Columbia University, checking references. Benji

Faradeux attended Columbia from 1968 to 1970. He was dismissed for leading an antiwar demonstration that caused significant property damage. Grant Wilder and Rosalynn Carter—no relation to Jimmy—were there in '69 and '70. They were very active in the same group."

"Motive?"

"Benji wants the company. Daddy promised it to Nanci."

"That's enough." Eileen twirled a pencil in her hand and asked, "What are you going to tell Faradeux?"

"As little as possible. I don't want Faradeux to blow it. Jacob would kill Benji, then he'd go after Nanci for not sharing her suspicions. Would you sit in on this meeting? I might need help."

A knot of tension was growing at the base of my skull. I kneaded it and finished my grim report. "There's more bad news: Wina Blake's missing." I told Eileen the pitiful story of how Wina snuck out of my house while Dennis and I were amusing ourselves in my bedroom, ending with "Welcome back."

Jona's soft knock on the door interrupted us before Eileen could dispense any wisdom. She stuck her head in and announced, "Mr. and Ms. Faradeux have arrived. They're waiting in the conference room."

Eileen dropped the pencil and stood up. "One problem at a time. We'll find the girl later."

I lagged to make a quick call to the hospital to see if Wina had appeared. She hadn't, and Grammie was still sleeping. I tried the school again, using a number I found in Grammie's address book. The woman who answered repeated what I'd been told earlier: "You want the truth, honey? We don't know who's here and who ain't here. We can't keep count—too many kids don't show up." I picked up a legal pad to look official and went to meet Faradeux, father and daughter.

JACOB AND NANCI were sitting at the table in the conference room, facing Eileen. Jacob was entertaining my sister by lecturing her on the fine points of castrating bulls. Nanci ignored her father's description and Eileen's uncomfortable squirming, preferring to concentrate on chewing her fingernails. Jacob stood when I entered the room and vigorously shook my hand.

"Hello, Red. Your sister here tells me you have good news. Must be good news for you to come in here dressed like one of my ranch hands."

I grimaced; I didn't need his ungentle dig about my attire. My day-old clothes felt wrinkled and stale; I hoped they didn't smell. Jacob pumped my hand again. "Now, Red, don't take that as an insult. You look comfortable and I'm jealous 'cause I'm wearing city clothes. I'm glad somebody in this here town has some horse sense—"

"Daddy—"

"Nanci means 'Sit down and shut up, you old fool.' Let's get down to business, Red. I've been telling Missy here all about running a ranch."

Missy glared at me. Even with one eye covered it was still an effective glare. I grinned at her. We were even for all the grief she'd caused me during the past week.

"I know you don't have time to idle around talking. My big shindig is coming up on Monday. Tell me what's going on."

"Your shindig should go off without any trouble." I sounded much more confident than I felt. "WARM is planning a demonstration outside the building. My staff has informed the NYPD and the Exchange about WARM's plans. They're ready to break it up."

Jacob accepted my optimistic report and relaxed. Trouble came from an unexpected source. Nanci stopped chewing on her fingernails and asked, "What about inside the Exchange? Is WARM planning anything to stop Daddy from ringing that gong?"

I thought of Grant's promise of a surprise and tried to answer confidently. "They will try to disrupt trading. I know some of their plan, I'm working on getting the rest of it."

"Red, you don't have much time."

"Today's Friday. I have until Monday."

EILEEN AND I HELD a somber postmeeting conference in my office. We settled into the comfortable corner and lit cigarettes. After spending a few minutes mimicking Jacob's Texas drawl, Eileen jumped to business.

"I hate to quote that insufferable cowboy, but he's right. You don't have much time."

"Now, don't you worry, Missy." Eileen frowned. I dropped my attempt at humor and said, "I promise, I'll call the Exchange early Monday morning with either fact or rumor. They'll investigate. Faradeux won't have his gong show until they're positive there aren't any explosives, or red paint, hidden in the place."

Eileen was quiet for a few seconds. She took a deep drag on her cigarette, blew out a cloud of smoke, and voiced the question she always asks: "What are you going to do?"

My answer was always the same. "I don't know."

TWENTY-ONE

WHERE WAS WINA? The question bothered me all afternoon. Eileen worked at my desk; I sat on the sofa and scribbled case notes, occasionally glancing at Eileen to check her progress. When I wasn't checking Eileen, I stared at the minute hand as it crept around the face of my watch.

Three fifty-seven. Enough time for Wina to have finished classes, if she had gone to school, and made her way to the office. Time to admit she wasn't going to show up. Three fifty-eight. The phone rang. Eileen answered it, listened for a few seconds, and asked the caller to hold.

She held the receiver out. "It's for you. Tony Parker."

"He's probably calling to chew me out about something I didn't do. He hasn't yelled at me for a day or two." I took the telephone and said hello.

"Blaine, how are you?"

"I'm fine, Tony. How are you?" Eileen smirked. I turned away and politely said, "What can I do for you? Is this business or pleasure?"

"Unfortunately, it's business. I have a little girl sitting outside my office who claims she's living with you. I thought I'd do you a favor and call instead of shipping her off to juvenile detention."

"Wina—"

"Yeah, that's her. Charming girl—are you teaching her manners? She curses at anybody who walks too close to her."

I let the insult go unanswered and matched the light-hearted lilt of Tony's voice. "What dastardly crime did she commit?"

"The girl was flashing a gun around her school-yard and the principal called the cops. The girl mentioned you were acting as temporary next of kin. Lucky for her, my guys recognized your name."

"Shit."

I was thinking about various methods of killing the child and didn't realize I had breathed my reaction into the phone. Tony chuckled. "My kids drove me crazy when they were teenagers. Why don't you come down and pick her up? Professional courtesy—it'll save us a lot of time."

"Thanks, Tony. I appreciate your help. See you in about half an hour."

I turned back to Eileen. She took the receiver from me, replaced it in its cradle, and laughed. "Has Parker become a good guy again?"

"I guess so." I relayed the half of the conversation she hadn't heard, tossing papers into my briefcase while I talked. "I'm going to try to get some work done at home tonight. How do you convince a six-teen-year-old that a gun won't solve her problems?"

Eileen shrugged. "Do you want an answer or a philosophical discourse on gun control?"

"No time for either. I have to go claim the kid." I slammed one last file into my briefcase and closed it. "Will you be here tomorrow?"

Eileen laughed. "What a ridiculous question. Of course I'll be here. See you tomorrow. Be careful."

FROM THE OUTSIDE, the 49th Precinct looks like a castle surrounded by a moat of cracked and littered sidewalk. Once visitors have successfully negotiated the broken pavement and the crumbling steps, they enter the soot-covered fortress, expecting to find King Arthur and a bunch of knights. A grungy interior filled with battered desks and plastic chairs shatters the castle illusion. Not a single knight in shining armor is visible.

The desk sergeant looked down from his lofty perch. He listened to my story and pointed to a staircase behind him. "Elevator's busted, you gotta walk."

Wina was sitting on a bench in the hallway. Relief spread across her face when she saw me approach but quickly faded when she saw the grim look on my face. I pointed to the bench. "Don't move. I have to thank the captain for letting you off. We'll talk when we get home."

Parker's office was filled with cops. Not wanting to interrupt, I waved at him through the open door and turned away. Tony left the cops gathered around his desk and rushed out after me.

"Sorry, I didn't want to break into your meeting. I wanted to thank you for calling me."

Precinct commanders don't have to obey the No Smoking signs on the walls. Tony lit a cigar and dropped the match to the floor. "You didn't interrupt anything, those guys are organizing our annual picnic. I needed a break from deciding major questions like how many hot dogs we need. Tell me some-

thing, when did you get into the baby-sitting business?
I don't picture you as the maternal type."

Parker was doing me a favor, so I smiled at his
comment about my maternal instincts. "The kid's
grandmother keeled over in my office the other day.
At first the doctors thought she had a stroke, now they
say it was stress—which doesn't surprise me, Wina's a
handful. The grandmother will be out of the hospital
tomorrow. I'll be very happy to get rid of my houseguest."

Tony guided me down the hallway. "Let's go take a
look at your little criminal. Maybe I can scare the shit
out of her so she doesn't pull a stunt like this again."

Wina hadn't moved from the bench; she was still
sullenly glaring at everyone who walked past. We
stopped in front of her, and I made the introductions.

"Tony, this is Wina Blake. Wina, Captain Parker is
in charge here. He's the reason why you aren't standing in front of a judge."

Parker yanked the cigar from his mouth and pulled
me away from the girl. "Is that the same Blake as
Hurley Blake?" I nodded. Tony exploded. "Jesus
Christ, are you still on that rag? I thought you were
done with that garbage."

"Tony, I—"

"Take the girl and get the hell out of here. Don't
come around looking for any more favors."

"Tony, listen to me."

"I'm not interested in your crap. I've had enough of
you and your attempts to get me." Parker pointed his
cigar at Wina. "You made your choice, now take it
home with you."

We left. We made a quick stop in a grocery store, then headed home. Wina didn't argue, explain, or apologize. It didn't take a sensitive genius to realize that talking to me would be a mistake. She followed a step behind, wisely letting me walk off my anger.

I marched into the kitchen, Wina trailing behind. Mikey yapped in the background as I took food from the bag and threw it on the table, working hard to get my temper under control. Wina glanced at the wok I took from a cabinet and complained.

"You Chinese? Grammie never stir-fry nothing."

I threw a package of mushrooms across the kitchen to her. "Cut these up, will you? Stop whining, you'll appreciate stir-fry when you get to the dishes—it only takes one pot." I started cutting the chicken. "This is the last night you have to eat strange food. Your grandmother is probably going to cook all your favorite food tomorrow to celebrate her homecoming."

"She better. I want hamburgers. And potatoes. And..." She paused, clumsily hacked at a mushroom, and innocently asked, "You mad at me?"

"Furious." I viciously whacked the chicken breast into small pieces. "You ran off this morning without letting me know where you were going. I wasted hours searching for you and worrying about you."

I whacked the chicken again. "Where did you get the money for the gun? Did you steal from me? Should I check my wallet to see if any money is missing? Or did you hock my silver?" I slammed the knife into another chicken breast. "What the hell are you trying to do?"

"That cop. What's his name?"

Facing each other with sharp knives wasn't a good idea; I was tempted to use mine for something worse than dissecting a chicken. I dropped the knife onto the cutting board and turned to the teenager. "Listen to me. I want an explanation of what you were doing today. Start with why you bought another gun."

Wina ignored my question and pretended to concentrate on slicing mushrooms; I was too angry to press for an answer. Telling myself she would be gone in the morning and I could forget the entire Blake family, I slammed the chicken into the wok, added mushrooms, broccoli, too much garlic, and ginger. A glob of hoisin sauce completed my masterpiece. I thawed some rice in the microwave and dumped my nameless Chinese creation over it. Dinner was ready. Wina took a bite and gulped the food down without chewing. She dropped her fork and stared at me.

"Now what's your problem?"

"Nothing."

Wina speared a piece of chicken, popped it into her mouth, and slowly chewed. She finally swallowed. "I cut school today—"

"I know. I looked for you." Telling myself that it didn't matter because the kid would be out of my hair in the morning, I said, "Why did you cut school?"

"I went home. I wanted to make things nice for Grammie." Was this the same kid who was getting busted for buying guns, intending to kill the people responsible for her father's death? "I looked around her room. She had some of Daddy's stuff—I know she told you she burned it, but I found it."

"What did you find?"

"A book. It has lots of names in it.... His name was there."

"Parker's name?" The girl nodded. "Are you sure Parker's name is in that book?"

"Yeah. It said he owed Daddy money. What's it mean?"

The girl was trying to hang on to an image of her father as a good guy and I wasn't going to destroy it. I ignored her question. "Where's the book?"

"It's in school, in my locker. I was afraid someone would try to take it."

The telephone rang. Wina ran across the kitchen and grabbed the receiver. "Yo, who's this?"

I winced and walked over to take the phone from her before she could do any more damage. "Hello."

"Stewart?"

I vaguely recognized the man's voice but couldn't connect it to a face. Wina went back to the table and shoved another load of food into her mouth, carefully listening to me as she chewed.

"Yes, this is Blaine. Who's this?"

"MacIntyre. You still looking for guys trying to buy bombs? 'Cause I got something. You interested?"

"What did you hear?"

"Couple guys made a connection last night. They was in Billy's this afternoon, drinking beers and carrying on 'bout this big job. I thought they was too drunk to do any big job so I called them on it. They said they had plenty of time to dry out. They gonna set it up tonight." Rudy paused for dramatic effect. "They gonna blow up the stock market."

Aware of Wina's prying ears, I casually asked, "What else did they say?"

"The cleanup crew gets done at nine. They use an entrance on New Street, in the back of the building. When they leave, they gonna leave the door open. These guys was bragging 'bout giving the security guards Christmas bundles big enough to buy enough blow so they wouldn't recognize Santa Claus comin' down the chimney. These guys will be in at nine, out by nine-thirty. Monday morning—boom. You gonna pay me?"

My mercenary informer anxiously waited for my response. "Let me check it out. If your information is good, you'll get paid. Call me tomorrow."

"When you going down there?"

"Don't worry, I'll check it out. If you're right, I'll pay you."

"Good." I heard a sigh of relief, then a click. The line disconnected.

Wina pushed some food around on her plate and asked, "You going out?"

Doesn't anyone speak in complete sentences anymore? I answered her question in very proper English. "Yes, I am going out later. I won't be gone very long." Long enough to see if Grant had more than red paint in mind for Jacob Faradeux.

I tried to finish dinner but my appetite was completely gone, replaced by whirling thoughts of how to prepare for my trip to the stock market. Still trying to be a good role model, I politely excused myself and ran upstairs to make calls in the privacy of my bedroom.

Eileen didn't answer. I cursed her unwillingness to use an answering machine and tried calling Dennis and Brad. Answering machines greeted me at each number. I cursed the unanswered phones and made a decision: beepers. The entire office was going to get beepers in the morning. I dialed Dennis again, impatiently waited for his message to end, then left a brief message before slamming the phone down in frustration. I called Brad's machine and left the same message.

It was almost eight-thirty. I was running out of time, I wanted to be at the exchange in time to catch Grant in the act of placing explosives. I hurried to dress in my combat outfit—dark jeans, blouse and jacket, sneakers, holster, gun, and extra ammunition clips— and sat at the desk. Puffing one last nervous cigarette before leaving, I wrote a short list of phone numbers for Wina.

When the list was finished, I went back down to the kitchen. My guest hadn't bothered to clean up. Dirty dishes were stacked on the counter next to the sink, while Wina sat at the table bent over another textbook. I interrupted the study session to give her the list. I carefully explained her role; a flicker of understanding passed through her eyes. Satisfied she would follow through, I ran from the house. It wasn't until I was in the car on the way to Wall Street that I thought to wonder how MacIntyre had gotten my home telephone number.

TWENTY-TWO

I PARKED a few blocks away from the Exchange and jogged to New Street. It wasn't hard to find a place to leave the car because Wall Street turns into a ghost town at night. All the traders, clerks, and support staff pack themselves into subways and PATH trains shortly after trading ends to go home and recover for the next day's battles, leaving behind thousands of parking places.

The public entrance to the New York Stock Exchange, the heart of Wall Street, isn't on Wall Street; it's on Broad Street. But I wasn't going to use the front door. I hurried past Broad Street and went around to the back.

I looked at the street sign and nodded. At least I had the answer to my geography question—I found New Street; it ran along the backside of the Exchange. Finding the right door was simple. It was midway down the short block—the one whose overhead security camera dangled uselessly from its wall brackets.

My nerves started tingling as soon as I touched the door. It wasn't locked. I pulled the door open, slipped inside, and waited to be challenged by a security guard. Silence was the only thing I heard.

I wandered around for a few minutes, peeking into storage rooms, janitor's closets, and bathrooms before finding the tunnel that led to the main arena. No one stopped me.

My stomach twisted. It was easy. Too easy. Too close to MacIntyre's script. I ignored my nerves and hurried through the passageway to a dark corner of the trading floor where I stood gulping air, telling myself I was waiting for my eyes to adjust to the darkness.

Everyone has seen pictures of the Stock Exchange when it's crowded with buyers and sellers. It's different at night when you stand on the edge of the quiet floor imagining the bedlam that would erupt if a bomb exploded during Jacob Faradeux's opening ceremony. Years of accumulated dirt turned the overhead skylights into opaque decorations, but my imagination provided enough light.

The rows of dark islands, the booths where the traders worked, would be filled with clerks ready to mark orders. The aisles would be crowded with specialists and floor brokers milling around, making last-minute jokes before the gong signaled the start of another workday. Jacob would be standing on the VIP balcony looking down at the crowd, a proud smile on his face. Nanci, Exchange officials, and the investment bankers would also be there. Everyone would be smiling. The smiles would disappear moments after Jacob drew back his arm.

I shook my head and thought about bombs. WARM wanted to do more than destroy Jacob Faradeux, they wanted to make a statement. The bomb would be at the weakest point: against the pillar that supported the VIP gallery. Grant wouldn't miss; the blast would bring the entire structure crashing to the floor. Chunks of concrete, splintered wood, and mangled bodies would cover the floor.

I shivered. My fingers touched the Smith & Wesson tucked in my jacket pocket and I felt a little more confident. I slid the pistol from my pocket and felt even better.

My meager supply of confidence evaporated when I looked across the room. It was a long way to the other side of the floor. Twenty feet of empty space stretched between the protective shadows where I was huddling and the first row of trading stations. A quick two-step across the dark floor would bring me to their shelter. From there I could hopscotch from booth to booth until I reached the balcony. I took a deep breath, held it for a second before exhaling, then pushed away from my safe corner.

If Eileen had been around, she would have quoted Homer to me: "Zeus does not bring all men's plans to fulfillment."

My plan didn't come close to fulfillment. I was several feet away from my first haven when a burst of gunfire sounded. My leg buckled and I crashed to the ground. The impact jarred the automatic from my hand. Fighting down the panic I was feeling, I groped along the floorboards, searching for the gun. My fingers brushed against the pistol grip just as another salvo flew overhead. I grabbed the gun and rolled onto my back, firing the entire clip as I moved.

Luck, not skill, guided my shots. A man screamed an obscenity, then he was quiet. An eerie silence fell over the room. I held my breath, listening vainly for footsteps.

The overhead lights flickered once, then came to life. I scrambled on my hands and knees into the nearest booth and crouched near the center column.

A dark stain spread across my right thigh as blood seeped into the denim. I quickly stripped off my jacket, wrapped it around my leg, and told myself to forget it. I had other worries.

Ammunition first. I replaced the clip in my automatic with a fresh one and put the backup into my shirt pocket. Thirty-two rounds. Against how many?

A familiar voice shouted, "Blaine! Where are you? Come on out."

Tony Parker. Short-lived relief overcame me; Parker's next words washed it away. "We got all night. MacIntyre got rid of the guards. He's good. You sure believed his story. But I knew you'd rush down here. You were always too impatient to wait for backup."

Parker was walking closer as he talked. I hugged my knees to my chest and tried to make myself small enough to hide under the counter. Hiding under counters isn't my usual style but my options were limited. I tried to think while Tony tried to talk me out into the open.

"MacIntyre and I made a deal. After tonight, I don't care what he does to your sister. Should be easy, getting rid of a one-eyed lady once her guardian angel is gone."

I clamped my mouth shut, holding back the curses I wanted to shout. The footsteps stopped outside my hiding place. With false concern, he said, "Blood. You're hurt." Parker's head appeared above the counter; he wasn't smiling. He pointed his service revolver at me and said, "Come on. Get out of there."

"Fuck you. Kill me here."

Parker shot. The computer monitor that was hanging behind me exploded, releasing a volley of sparks, broken glass, and bits of plastic. My former mentor lowered the barrel of his gun and aimed it at my head. His finger slowly compressed the trigger.

"Go ahead, Tony. Kill me. Just like you killed Hurley Blake. But before you do it, give me a reason I can understand. You owe me that much."

Tony's bloodshot eyes avoided mine as he calmly told his story. My leg was throbbing and I could see blood oozing through the makeshift bandage. I forced myself to remain still and concentrate on not drawing Parker's attention to the gun hidden behind my drawn-up legs.

"Blake was squeezing me. I should have killed him right away but I didn't. I thought I could scare him away by applying pressure. It didn't work. Every time I busted him, he called your sister and I had to back off."

I quietly asked, "Why did you kill him?"

Parker's voice rose. "The last time I busted him, he got mad, told me he was going to squeal to the newspapers about the raid. I would have lost my job, my promotion, my pension—everything. When you started asking questions, I had to stop you. I used the leftovers from Blake's storeroom."

The raid. An uneasy memory, one I'd been trying to deny, stirred inside my head. I interrupted Parker's apology for accidentally killing Ida. "Jeff's notebook has you listed as the NYPD liaison." A sick hole opened in my stomach. "Oh God. You did it...."

Parker didn't answer. He didn't have to speak, I saw the truth in his ashen face. The gun drooped slightly.

"Why..." My voice cracked. I licked my lips and tried again. "Why did you do it?"

He wouldn't look at me; I wanted to see his eyes. "I made some bad bets. I owed money—a lot of money. Leaking the arrangements was the only way out."

My muscles tensed, my heart pounded. Parker's admission was a mistake: now that I had found the traitor who killed my husband, I would do anything to kill him. An enemy who isn't afraid to die is a very dangerous enemy.

The sound of running feet echoed through the chamber. Dennis's voice called, "Blaine? Are you in here? Answer me—where are you?"

Parker wasn't distracted by the outcry. He slowly lifted his revolver.

We fired simultaneously. My shot was the first to arrive at its target. Parker dropped, hitting the floor with a hearty thunk; his shot grazed my shoulder and buried itself in a stack of order tickets. I gently laid my pistol on the floor and closed my eyes. I've seen enough corpses to know that Parker was dead.

TWENTY-THREE

I WOKE in a quiet hospital room, feeling almost normal. My first visitor smothered my feelings of enthusiasm.

Harold Hodgkins, formally dressed in a dark suit, crisp white shirt, and government-approved dark tie, walked into the room. He wasn't smiling. Hodgkins flashed a plastic-coated ID card and sat; the card said he didn't need an invitation.

Hodgkins was unhappy; his dour eyes stared at me. I stared back, surprised to learn he was one of the good guys, but I wasn't going to admit it.

"The antiterrorism unit spent a lot of time on WARM. You almost blew our case."

"I don't agree. From my side of the desk, it looked as if you weren't making any progress." Hodgkins frowned. I finished making him angry by asking, "Am I being charged with something? Should I call my attorney?"

Hodgkins pursed his lips and looked out the window. "Based on the information you passed to Halstead and the results of my investigation, we were issued a search warrant for WARM's office. We found pressure-sensitive detonators, explosives, and plans. Detonation would have occurred when Faradeux opened trading. We also found a large quantity of C-4, wrapping paper, and timing mechanisms—preliminary testing matches everything to the fragments from the bomb in your sister's office.''

"What about Roz and Grant?"

Hodgkins smiled. "Roz is blaming Wilder. He won't talk. We'll be able to make a strong conspiracy case against them. They left a lot of handwritten plans in the office.''

"How did you get Dennis pulled off the investigation?" I tried to keep my voice calm and professional, something I hadn't been able to do when Dennis had delivered the news.

"You looked familiar but I couldn't place you. I wandered into Halstead's office one day to pick up a report and saw your picture on his desk. I pulled rank and got him assigned to something else.''

I frowned. Hodgkins nodded his agreement. "Coincidence—I didn't like it either. I didn't want to compromise my investigation. So I got him reassigned.''

Paranoid behavior didn't end with J. Edgar Hoover's death. Rather than repeat the nasty thoughts in my mind, I just smiled.

Hodgkins continued. "Ben Faradeux was supplying WARM with money. Unfortunately, he was overdrawn on his allowance. That's why they were encouraging you to fill their empty checkbook.''

A slight grin of admiration crossed his face. "You did a good job burying information about yourself. I had a hard time getting a line on you.''

And, of course, he wouldn't ask Dennis. Instead of pointing out the obvious, I asked, "What happened to Benji Faradeux?"

Hodgkins shook his head. "Unfortunately, donating money to a charitable organization isn't a crime. We don't have enough evidence to nail him. He'll get off."

I imagined Jacob's wrath. "Benji won't get off. Jacob Faradeux will torture him forever. Jail would have been easier for Benji to deal with."

THE BLOOD LOSS from my leg had frightened me, but the wound wasn't serious. The bullet had missed the femur, missed the artery, and carved a narrow furrow through a lot of muscle. With luck, it wouldn't leave much of a scar. The scratch on my shoulder was gone in days.

I was back at work in a week. Most of my work was done on the sofa in my office with my leg resting gingerly on a pillow. I never complained—I was happy to be working again, happy to be reading boring reports and directing staff investigations.

Late in the afternoon on my third day back, Eileen strolled into my office carrying a thick folder under her arm. I put my papers aside and watched her cautiously navigate the narrow channel between the sofa and table, concentrating on placing her feet in the proper spots. Eileen's flawed depth perception still occasionally betrayed her, causing her to stumble gracelessly and rudely thrust aside helping hands.

Eileen made it without incident and sat at the end of the sofa. She pushed my feet aside and said, "A check came from Faradeux Industries today. He included a Texas-sized bonus and an invitation to visit his ranch in Texas."

She passed the folder to me. "Here's your file. I just got back from the district attorney's office—you're in business again." She took a cigarette from the pack on the table and lit it. "You've been cleared. They're going to drop the charges."

I held my hand out for the cigarettes and lit one for myself. "They should have given me a medal instead of yanking my license." On the morning following the shootout, while I was in the hospital sleeping off the effects of surgery, my license had been suspended "pending an investigation." It would be a long time before I would have kind thoughts about anyone in that office. "I still don't understand why they lifted my license."

Eileen sighed. "You shot up the floor of the New York Stock Exchange. They found Parker dead, Duke with a hole in his chest, and MacIntyre hiding in a closet. For God's sake, Blaine, there were bullet holes in the booth where they trade IBM—you can't shoot holes in Big Blue and not expect an uproar." She laughed. "Fortunately you have a good attorney. I convinced them that arresting you would be a mistake."

"How did you persuade them I wasn't a dangerous criminal?"

"Dennis helped. He got there just in time to be your star witness. Dennis got your message, then Wina called and insisted that he get down there. He gathered the troops to storm the Exchange."

Eileen put her head back and blew a perfect smoke ring. I watched enviously; I had never mastered smoke rings. "Dennis is convinced you shot Parker in self-defense. The D.A.'s office believed him. It's hard to doubt his sincere FBI voice." She blew another smoke ring and innocently asked, "It was self-defense, wasn't it?"

Eileen's question startled me; it was one I asked myself a hundred times a day. I blinked and said, "What are you talking about?"

"The indulgence of revenge tends to make men more savage and cruel. Lord Kames, a Scottish lawyer and philosopher, said that in the 1700s. Were you indulging your revenge?"

"Parker killed Jeff. I wanted to kill Parker. But I couldn't do it." Eileen's gaze was relentless. I looked at my cigarette and quickly ground it out in the ashtray. "Dennis is right. It was self-defense. Tony tried to kill me. I shot back."

Eileen gently patted my leg—the good one. "We both got beat up on this one. Give yourself a break, you'll be okay."

Good advice. Hard to follow.

EPILOGUE

THERE'S A Bruce Springsteen song with lyrics that ask, "Is a dream a lie if it don't come true, or is it something worse?" Well, I found something worse: a dream that does come true. Dreams of revenge had sustained me after Jeff's death; now they haunted me.

I was drawn to Battery Park that summer. In good weather and bad, I'd limp around the southern tip of Manhattan, pausing to stare across the water at the Statue of Liberty, looking for answers. When Lady Liberty remained silent, I'd limp on, dodging the tourists hurrying for the ferry.

Dennis joined me whenever he could squeeze the time from his overbooked schedule. I didn't do much walking on those days. Never listening to my protestations about the need for exercise, Dennis always insisted that we sit and rest my leg. He'd buy hot dogs from a sidewalk vendor and we'd sit on a bench facing the water, letting the salty wind blow across our faces as we ate. Circling sea gulls happily caught our leftovers in midair.

Dennis and I tried to fall in love again that summer. We're still trying, but my dreams get in the way. I still wake up in the middle of the night, covered with sweat and wondering. If only the nightmares would stop.

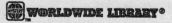

FOUR ON THE FLOOR

RALPH McINERNY

A Father Dowling Mystery Quartet

First Time in Paperback

THE FEROCIOUS FATHER
Mr. O'Halloran had lots of fund-raising ideas for
St. Hilary's—plus an unidentified corpse in his car
trunk. Had the Mob followed Mr. O'Halloran to town?

HEART OF COLD
Branded a thief, old Ray has paid his debt to society.
But when he is abducted, Father Dowling must prove
that crime is all in the family.

THE DEAD WEIGHT LIFTER
A body is deposited at St. Hilary's, and Father Dowling
must find out who the man is and why he died.

THE DUTIFUL SON
Father Dowling agrees to help a man by exhuming
and reburying the body of an infant who died years
ago. But the body in question proves to be something
quite different.

"Excellent short adventures, crisply written, with
surprising twists."   —*St. Louis Post-Dispatch*

Available in October at your favorite retail stores.

The **DOWN HOME** *Heifer Heist*

Eve K. SANDSTROM

A Sam & Nicky Titus Mystery

THIN ICE

Rancher Joe Pilkington, neighbor to Sheriff Sam Titus and photographer wife Nicky, is run down when he interrupts rustlers during a heist. Aside from tire tracks in the snow, the only clue is the sound of Mozart heard playing from the killer's truck.

Two more grisly deaths follow, and it looks as if a beloved member of the Titus ranch may be accused of murder. Sam and Nicky grimly set out to corner a killer...before they become victims themselves.

"Sandstrom makes the most of her setting...."
— *Publishers Weekly*

Available in October at your favorite retail stores.

 WORLDWIDE LIBRARY®

HEIFER